Eldritch Manor

Eldritch Manor

Kim Thompson

DUNDURN
TORONTO

Project Editor: Michael Carroll
Editor: Allister Thompson
Design: Jennifer Scott
Printer: Webcom

Library and Archives Canada Cataloguing in Publication

Thompson, Kim, 1964-
    Eldritch Manor / Kim Thompson.

Issued also in electronic formats.
ISBN 978-1-4597-0354-4

    I. Title.

PS8639.H6276E44 2012   jC813'.6   C2011-908012-5

1   2   3   4   5   16   15   14   13   12

Conseil des Arts   Canada Council   Canada   ONTARIO ARTS COUNCIL
du Canada   for the Arts   CONSEIL DES ARTS DE L'ONTARIO

We acknowledge the support of the Canada Council for the Arts and the Ontario Arts Council for our publishing program. We also acknowledge the financial support of the Government of Canada through the Canada Book Fund and Livres Canada Books, and the Government of Ontario through the Ontario Book Publishing Tax Credit and the Ontario Media Development Corporation.

Visit us at
Dundurn.com | Definingcanada.ca | @dundurnpress | Facebook.com/dundurnpress

Dundurn	Gazelle Book Services Limited	Dundurn
3 Church Street, Suite 500	White Cross Mills	2250 Military Road
Toronto, Ontario, Canada	High Town, Lancaster, England	Tonawanda, NY
M5E 1M2	LA1 4XS	U.S.A. 14150

To my writing group, for kind words

And to my daughter Lizzie,
For everything else
[xoxo]

Chapter One

In which our heroine goes out to seek her fortune in the world, but finds only old ladies and scrapes her knees

As she tumbled over the handlebars of her bike, twelve-year-old Willa Fuller decided that this had to be the absolute worst day of her life so far.

It was the first day of summer vacation, a day she'd been eagerly anticipating for months. The sun shone down on her small town, the birds sang, the children played, but Willa was in a "slough of despond" (a lovely phrase she'd read somewhere). And falling off her bike was the least of her troubles. Everything had gone wrong from the very start of her day.

At breakfast her bread got caught in the toaster and burned and smoked and stank up the whole kitchen. Then her mom came in, waving aside the smoke without comment, which was a sign something grim was in the offing.

"Something grim is in the offing," announced Willa, because she liked saying old-fashioned words like that, but also to make her mom smile. Her mom did not smile. Another bad sign.

"Willa," she said flatly, "you won't be staying with Grandpa this summer." Grandpa lived in a tiny house right on the ocean, and every summer Willa went to stay with him for two or three weeks. She looked forward to it all year. Just a short drive from town, the seashore seemed like another world. At Grandpa's she didn't have to worry about being cool or popular, she could read all day if she liked, or wander up and down the beach looking for treasures, and she always, always found something good. But what she liked most of all was that Grandpa always treated her like a grown-up.

"Is he all right?" Willa asked anxiously.

Her mom smiled, nodding. "Grandpa's fine, don't worry."

Willa hated "serious" talks like this. You just didn't know what terrible thing was coming next. Her mom looked down at the table and went on.

"It's just that things aren't going so well, and we thought maybe you could get a summer job here in town and help out."

Willa was stunned. All she could do was nod as her stomach turned right over. Things not going well? Were they broke? She guessed it had to do with Grandpa. He himself admitted he was the worst fisherman in the world. He said his good luck had left him the same time Willa's grandmother had, long ago when Willa's mom was still young. Whatever the reason, while his friends hauled in catch after catch of wriggling fish, Grandpa's nets always came up empty. He now made his living by renting his boat to tourists and fixing traps and nets for the other fishermen. It wasn't much of a living, and Willa knew Mom and Dad sent him money to keep him going.

Willa stared down at her burnt toast as all this ran through her mind. She wished Dad was there to back her up, but he'd already left for work. Her mother briskly brushed the toast crumbs from the table. "Don't your friends work in the summer? I always had a job when I was your age."

Willa shook her head. "They go to camp mostly. Nicky's at camp, Flora's at camp. Kate's at the cottage with her cousins." It wasn't her friends' fault they went away for the summer, Willa knew, but she still felt abandoned.

Her mother barely registered what she'd said. "Well, anyway ... I'd like you to go see Hattie at the *Tribune* today. She said she'd try to find a job for you there. Delivering papers at least. It's not much but it'll be a start." Her mom rose, smiling. "Your first job! Isn't that exciting?" And she breezed out of the kitchen, not waiting for an answer, and not registering the utterly miserable look on Willa's face.

So on what should have been a gloriously free first day of summer, Willa unhappily pedalled over to the newspaper office. Climbing the front steps she caught sight of her reflection in the glass door. She looked so awkward, all bony knees and skinny arms, in second-hand clothes that didn't fit properly. Her curly hair stuck out in all directions. And to top it all off she was slouching, which always made her mom yell at her. She made a face. Then she thought about Grandpa, took a deep breath, pulled herself up straight, and went inside.

9

The newspaper office filled her with dread. It was easy for her mom to talk about getting a job, like it was the simplest thing in the world, but dealing with strangers, especially grown-ups, just made Willa anxious. Her mother was calm, clear, and forceful, always in control, but Willa ... Willa panicked, Willa mumbled, Willa dropped things and stumbled over her own feet whenever someone was watching. Willa only felt comfortable when she was alone, reading and daydreaming. Or when she was with her grandpa at the seashore, but of course now that was off the agenda. Instead she was here in a loud and busy newspaper office full of vaguely alarming grown-ups.

Willa inched up to the front desk and asked for her Aunt Hattie. She had to ask four times because the receptionist couldn't hear her over the ringing phones and people talking. Aunt Hattie was Dad's older sister. She was tall, huge, really, with five or six pencils always stuck and forgotten in her frizzy hair. The same frizzy hair Willa had, from Dad's side of the family. Hair that did the opposite of what you wanted it to, that defied gravity, and doubled in volume whenever it rained.

Now Hattie and her hair emerged from her office and loomed over Willa. She had the scowl of a person who is very busy and wants you to know it. "Willa," she said flatly, "we've got all the carriers we need." Willa smiled with relief, but Hattie wasn't finished. "But I do have a spot in sales. It's commission work. That means you only make money if you sell subscriptions. Take it or leave it."

It didn't seem that "leave it" was really an option. Hattie didn't wait for an answer but loaded Willa up with sample papers, an order book, and a list of the addresses of people who didn't subscribe to the *Trilby Tribune* but should. It was now Willa's solemn duty to talk them into changing their ways.

As Willa loaded the papers into her bike carrier, she reflected gloomily on her fate. She hadn't even wanted to deliver papers, but now that seemed like the best job in the world compared to knocking on doors and talking to strangers all day.

From that low point the day proceeded in a downhill direction. As Willa covered street after street, rang doorbells, and gave away sample papers, it became increasingly apparent that she was a terrible salesperson. When she launched into her "sales pitch" her mouth dried up and her voice became so thin and quavery that no one could hear what she was saying. She had to repeat herself over and over until the words got all tangled and she sounded like an idiot.

After a full day pedalling around in the dust and heat, she hadn't sold a single subscription, and she only had one more house on her list. It was the big house backing onto the ravine, the old rambly one that was twice the size of all the other houses on the block. Willa used to imagine that someone fabulously wealthy and glamorous lived there, until her mom told her it was a rooming house for seniors. After that the old place just hadn't seemed so interesting anymore.

She paused in front under a weeping willow. There was a small sign on the gate that she'd never noticed before, obscured by vines. It said "Eldritch Manor." Willa

11

peered up at the house. It seemed too grand a name for such a tired-looking place, with its weathered, peeling paint and the porch sagging under its own weight. Still, the house had a kind of weary dignity, with its gabled windows and turrets and little balconies. There was even a widow's walk on the roof. The place sure had more character than her house, a boring modern little bungalow. She longed for a widow's walk. If they had one she'd be up there all day. She'd stare out toward the ocean and pace tragically. She'd pretend she was waiting for someone to return after years and years of agonizing separation. It would sure beat selling newspapers.

She climbed the front steps to the porch where two old ladies were snoozing in the sunshine. One was lying on a sofa, her round, smiling face tilted toward the sun and one short leg dangling. She was rather rotund and didn't so much lie on the sofa as flow across it, like she had no bones. An empty cat food tin was balanced on the arm of the sofa, which was scratched to ribbons, but there were no cats in sight.

The second lady sat in a wheelchair with a blanket covering her legs. Her beautiful silvery hair fell all the way to the floor behind her, glinting in the sunshine like tinsel. She too was a little large and fleshy, but her hands in her lap were long and narrow, and her face was thin and delicate. She would have been positively elegant had it not been for the snuffling, snorting, and wheezing issuing from her open mouth as she slept. Willa paused on the top step and cleared her throat. No one stirred. She tried again. "Excuse me? Hello?"

The round lady on the sofa opened one eye and squinted at her. "Hmmm?" she purred. Willa nervously started her pitch. "I'm here ... the *Trilby Tribune* ... you don't ... would you like ... I'm selling subscriptions...."

The lady didn't speak or even move, she just watched Willa with that one open eye, which made Willa even more nervous. She took a deep breath and started again.

"I'm selling subscriptions to the *Trilby Tribune*, would you like to subscribe?"

She held out a sample paper. The lady slowly closed the one eye and began to stretch, first one arm then the other, then a leg then the other leg ... all the while yawning great gaping yawns without even covering her mouth. Willa waited — what else could she do? Finally the old lady sat up straight and opened her eyes, both of them this time. She reached over and poked the lady in the wheelchair with one long, curved nail.

"Belle! Wake up! You're snoring again!"

Belle started awake, snorting a little. She scowled. "I do NOT snore, you mangy old beast!" Then she noticed Willa. Her face rolled back into a big smile and her voice smoothed into honey.

"A visitor. How lovely. Why didn't you wake me, Baz?" Baz snorted and rolled her eyes as she settled back onto the sofa. Belle gestured for Willa to come closer.

"I'm selling newspaper subscriptions, ma'am."

Belle didn't seem to hear her. She was too busy looking her up and down. Her stare grew more and more intense, and Willa felt a sudden chill. Belle's eyes were like marbles, all swirly blue and green. And Willa suddenly noticed how pale she was — white as a sheet, practically.

"I know you," the old lady finally announced, sitting back serenely. "I know you better than you know yourself." *Great*, thought Willa, *crazy lady alert*. She tried again. "Would you be interested in sub —"

"Tell me something, dearie," Belle interrupted, taking Willa's hand in her own, which was cool and smooth as a stone. She smiled sweetly. "Do you have a car?"

Eyes closed, Baz cautioned in a singsong tone, "Miss Trang will heeear youuuu."

Belle waved her off, but her voice dropped to a whisper as she leaned closer, fixing Willa with her watery eyes. "Do you have a car, sweetie? Could you take a helpless little old lady to the seashore?" She batted her long lashes.

Willa shook her head. "I don't — I can't drive. I'm only twelve."

Belle's mood changed once more. "Well, that's just great!" she snapped, dropping Willa's hand, her eyes now icy. Baz had leaned over and was sniffing at Belle's sleeve. Belle shook her off. "Stop it! For goodness sake!"

Baz curled up on the sofa again, smiling dreamily. "I can't help it. You smell so nice ... like tuna."

It was true, but Belle was outraged. "I do not, you fool!" she shot back.

"Do too!"

"Do not!"

"Do too!"

"Liar!"

14

"Fishy smelling fishy fish!"

"Fleabag!"

"LADIES!"

Willa jumped. A woman stood in the doorway, looking at them sternly. She was ... smooth. General impression, smooth. Willa couldn't tell how old she was — she seemed much older than Willa's mom but her skin was smooth, no wrinkles at all. Her hair was smoothed back into a bun. Her clothes, a very simple skirt and shirt, were dark grey, boring, and smooth.

"She started it," growled Belle, crossing her arms sulkily.

"I didn't. She called me a fleabag, Miss Trang." Baz gave Belle a smug smile. Belle stuck out her tongue. Miss Trang ignored them and turned to Willa.

"Who are you? What do you want?" Her voice rolled out effortlessly, like oil. Smooth. Willa couldn't even tell if she was being friendly or unfriendly.

"I'm ... um, selling ..."

Miss Trang cut her off brusquely. "We're not interested, but thank you for dropping by."

Willa looked back at the ladies. Belle was sulking. Baz seemed to be asleep.

"Goodbye," prompted Miss Trang. Definitely unfriendly now. Willa mumbled an awkward goodbye and hurried down the steps, just glad to be leaving. She picked up her bike and put the sample paper in the carrier. Zero sales. She was officially the worst salesperson in the world.

"Psst!"

Willa turned to see Belle waving her back, her bony fingers rippling through the porch railing. Miss Trang had disappeared inside, so Willa tiptoed through the flowerbed until she was directly below the old lady, who was smiling again.

"Darling child, do see if you can get me a ride to the seashore, will you please?"

"But I told you I —"

"Just try. I'm sure you can manage something. Give me your hand."

Willa held up her hand. Belle flicked her long white fingers and a stream of coins suddenly appeared, dribbling from her hand into Willa's. *Neat trick*, she thought.

"I can't take this," she protested, but Belle cut her off. "It's for that, whatever you're selling...."

"Newspapers."

"Yes, whatever. Now go on, before she sees you."

Willa needed no more prompting. She made a quick exit, dumping the coins into her pocket, where they now jangled as she fell forward over her handlebars, shortly after her front wheel hit the curb in front of the newspaper office, the one curb in town that is half an inch too high, which is precisely where we came in.

After a short, uneventful flight, she landed on the sidewalk, rolling and scraping her palms, elbows, and knees. She lay for a moment with her cheek on the hot pavement. Her eyes teared up. Her hands stung horribly but her first thought was — *did anyone see?*

She looked up and sure enough, just her luck, there were some grade nine boys across the street, outside the corner store. They were laughing. One of them said something she couldn't hear and the laughter doubled.

Willa blinked back tears as she sat up and inspected her palms. Why couldn't she have broken her leg? Then she could spend the summer in bed with a giant cast and read all day instead of getting a stupid job. Pulling up her left knee for a closer look, she heard some of the coins slip out of her pocket onto the sidewalk with a soft clink. She turned to see them rolling away, which immediately struck her as odd because they were rolling *uphill*. She quickly put out a foot to stop them.

The three coins abruptly stopped and executed a smart right hand turn, curving around her foot and continuing on their way up the sidewalk.

Chapter Two

As Willa pedalled home, she was no longer thinking about her scraped knees or stinging hands, or even about the boys who'd laughed at her. Normally when she did something embarrassing in front of people, she ran it over and over in her head until she wanted to scream. Not this time. All she could think about were the coins jingling in her pocket.

She wasn't even thinking about the stern look on Aunt Hattie's face when she told her aunt that she hadn't sold any subscriptions. Willa had decided to keep those wacky old ladies and their coins to herself.

"Maybe you're just not cut out for sales," Hattie had said. Willa couldn't agree more.

About a block from home she stopped and pulled out the whole fistful of change. It looked like a normal jumble of coins — none of them were covered in runes or anything, just the regular queen heads, beavers, sailboats, and elk. She was just wondering if she had hallucinated the whole thing when the coins began to jump in her hand. She slapped her other hand over them and they wriggled beneath it, tickling her palm and making her shiver. When they calmed down again she shoved them back in her pocket, all but one, which she placed on the sidewalk. She watched closely as it hopped up on its edge, slowly spun around a couple of times, and rolled off down the street.

Fifteen minutes later the coin slowed and made a sharp turn up the walkway of the big house. *Well, that makes sense,* thought Willa. *It's heading back to where it came from.* The porch was empty. The coin reached the bottom of the stairs and paused for a moment before *leaping* onto the first step. Willa stared as it jumped up all the stairs, then rolled right up and banged into the front door with a faint *ping!* In her pocket the rest of the coins suddenly went crazy, jumping and jiggling. She pulled them out and they fairly flew from her hands, thwacking themselves into the door over and over again.

Inside the house there was movement, footsteps, a cat's meow. Then the door swung open and the coins dropped lifeless at the feet of Miss Trang. She glared at Willa with dark, glittering eyes.

"What do you want?"

Willa froze under her cold stare. She had been so focussed on the coins she hadn't even considered what she would say once she got there. Baz peeked out from behind the woman's left shoulder, covering her mouth and laughing silently. Miss Trang glanced down at the coins and rolled her eyes.

"Belle!" she barked over her shoulder, sending Baz scampering away down the dark hall. Miss Trang turned back to Willa.

"Belle gave you some money. She probably wanted you to take her to the ocean, am I right?" Willa didn't know what to say. She didn't want to tell on anyone, so she kept quiet. Miss Trang continued. "And her money started acting strangely and here you are. You think the coins are *magic*. You want to solve the *mystery*." She was speaking very quickly and sharply. Willa backed away, feeling small and foolish. Miss Trang paused, her voice softening just a little, little bit.

"Well, there is no magic and there is no mystery. Belle was just playing a little trick with magnets. Nothing more." A teeny smile crawled across her face, but it wasn't reassuring ... it just made her look scary.

"And we don't want any newspapers. Goodbye." The last word was so firm and final that Willa could do nothing but turn and go down the steps. At the bottom she looked back to see Baz picking up the coins as Miss Trang held the door open.

As she reached the sidewalk she heard the door slam shut behind her. She glanced back and spotted Belle in an upstairs window, slowly combing her long, long hair. Willa could hear her humming mournfully and froze in her steps, overcome with sudden pangs of sorrow. She looked so sad. Willa waved but Belle was looking beyond her, gazing off in the direction of the ocean.

Willa's mind was racing. Magnets? Ridiculous. What magnets could work all the way across town? Miss

Trang was lying. What was going on in that house? Was she keeping those old ladies prisoner?

That evening Willa found her mom in the bathroom surrounded by tubes of colour, busily banishing the grey from her hair. Twisting her towel into a turban, Mom scowled to hear that Willa was giving up on the newspaper job. But Willa had a plan B. She would work doing odd jobs — mowing lawns, weeding, cleaning houses, pet-sitting, that kind of thing. She'd even made posters with their phone number at the bottom that she was going to put up all over the neighbourhood. Her mom was surprised for sure, maybe even impressed. When Willa showed the posters to her dad, he said she had gumption.

Willa herself felt uncommonly adventurous. Especially because of the secret motivation behind her plan B. The posters were really just a way to get another look at the old house by the park. Willa was going to get inside and try to find out more about its inhabitants. She felt excited and nervous at the same time. It was like real detective work! It might even be dangerous. Well, probably not very dangerous. After all, it was just bunch of little old ladies.

The next day she went about taping her posters to lampposts all over the neighbourhood. When she reached the park across from the old house, she sat on a bench, pulled out a book, and waited.

Detective work turned out to be more boring than she expected. The porch was empty and nothing happened for nearly two and a half hours. She had finished her book and was just nodding off when the slam of the front door snapped her awake. Miss Trang strode off down the street, purposefully consulting a piece of paper, a shopping bag slung over one arm. Willa held her book up in front of her face until the coast was clear, then she strolled casually to the front gate of the big house, her heart pounding. As she passed through the gate, something small and hard hit her on the head with a sharp CRACK!

An acorn dropped to the ground in front of her. Willa rubbed her head, wondering what acorns were doing falling from a willow tree. She peered up into the branches, right into an old, old face, brown and lined with wrinkles, all of them creased into a smirk.

"Gotcha!" it squealed.

Startled, Willa let out a shriek and jumped back as the owner of the face swung from a branch and landed heavily in front of her. He grimaced, clutching his back as he straightened up. Willa was surprised to find the old man was smaller than she was — he only came up to her shoulder, but he raised his fists as if to fight her.

"Wanna fight? Hmm? I may be old but I'm *wily!*" He danced, hopping awkwardly around her.

"I was just going to visit ..."

"Hah!" he interrupted, squinting at her. "Aren't you scared? I am Tengu, and this house is feared by all!" He hopped back and forth, grimacing and waving his arms. The effect wasn't very scary; in fact, it was all Willa could do to keep from laughing. She covered her smile with one hand, not wanting to hurt his feelings.

Then he stopped and leaned in conspiratorially. "I bet you've heard lots of scary stories about this place. Yes? Hm? Well ... they're *all true!*" With this he let out an exultant wolf howl. "OwWOOOOO!"

Willa looked around nervously. She really didn't want to attract any attention. "I — I haven't heard any stories at all," she admitted.

Tengu stopped in mid-howl, his face falling. He was clearly disappointed. "None? Doesn't anyone talk about this house?"

Willa shrugged helplessly. The little man's energy seemed to drain away. He plunked himself down cross-legged on the walk with his frowning head in his hands. "No reputation at all. Simply unacceptable. Something must be done," he muttered.

"There may be stories, I've just never heard them," Willa offered, but he waved her away, lost in thought. She stepped around him and continued up the porch steps, taking a deep breath. Back to her plan. She was going to find out what was going on and do her best to help those dear old ladies. Miss Trang couldn't keep them trapped in there. They'd be so glad that she'd come to rescue them.

Willa paused at the front door. She could hear voices inside, arguing loudly. She rang the bell. The voices stopped abruptly. There was a moment of silence and then the door opened a crack. Baz peered out through the chain, just staring at her, not speaking. Willa cleared her throat.

"Hm. Hello. I'm ... I was here the other day. Selling newspapers?"

Baz stared blankly at her. A long, uncomfortable moment passed. Willa felt it was now or never. She drew herself up to her full height and spoke in her best "Aunt Hattie voice," surprising even herself. "I want to talk to you about a very, *very* important matter!"

Baz pursed her lips and squinted. Willa squinted back. Finally Baz blinked. "Well ... hold on a sec."

She shut the door again and a great ruckus began inside — banging, a loud thumping up the stairs, more banging, whispered arguing. When all was quiet, Baz suddenly swung the door open, grabbed Willa by the arm, and yanked her inside, slamming the door after her.

Willa stumbled into the dark hall, dropping her posters. She stooped to pick them up, waiting for her eyes to adjust to the gloom. The place smelled distinctly of cat. She followed Baz into the parlour, where someone was shouting.

The room was dark, the sunshine blotted out by heavy red curtains. It was very old-fashioned and crazily cluttered, with leather armchairs and ottomans underfoot and a flowery sofa scuffed by cat claws. There was a fireplace, a piano, spidery plants on little end tables, a large dollhouse in the corner, ghostly white teacups on dark shelves, and doilies over the backs of the chairs. A large birdcage hung in one dark corner, housing some kind of bird, asleep with its head under its wing. More immediately, however, Belle and a distinguished old gentleman were shouting across the room at one another.

"You know-nothing pompous *ass!*" Belle barked.

"Loud-mouthed shrew!" the man hollered back, frowning behind tiny wire spectacles. Willa watched in alarm as Belle grabbed a teacup and hurled it at the man. He neatly deflected it with a throw cushion, sending it crashing into the piano. Baz didn't seem to mind the ruckus. Grinning, she draped herself on the sofa with her hands folded beneath her chin.

The man picked up a scone and lobbed it at Belle; she in turn grabbed another teacup.

"Stop! Stop!" Willa hollered. They turned, staring, and she felt herself blushing.

Belle dropped the cup onto an ottoman. "We have a visitor. Behave yourself, Horace."

The man straightened his tie and jacket, looking very tweedy and professorial. He sat back down as Belle swivelled her wheelchair to peer at Willa. "Who are you and what do you want?"

"I'm Willa. I was here the other day...." Blank look. "Selling newspapers?" Belle shrugged, tucking her blanket around her legs. Willa tried again. "You wanted me to take you to the ocean, remember?"

At this Belle's eyes lit up. Her face split into a grin. "Oh! and you've come to take me there. You dear, sweet, sweet girl!"

"No, I can't do that, exactly...."

Belle's face fell into a scowl. "Well, what good are you then?" This was it. Willa stepped forward.

"I've come to help you."

Horace sat up quickly. "Then settle this for us. Who do you think would win in a fight ... Odin or

Zeus?" Both he and Belle leaned forward, eagerly awaiting her answer.

Willa blinked in surprise. "You mean, the gods Odin and Zeus?" They nodded. "What kind of a fight?"

Belle answered, holding up her own bony fists. "A bare-knuckle brawl. No magic, no flying, no weapons, no outside help. Who would you bet on?" Willa thought it over carefully for a moment.

"I don't think they'd fight. Wouldn't it make more sense if it was Thor and Ares? The gods of war?"

The old man cackled. "You have a point there," he started, but was interrupted by a loud banging from upstairs. He shouted up at the ceiling. "She says they wouldn't fight!" He was answered by a loud crash that made Willa jump. Horace grinned. "Our distinguished colleague upstairs disagrees with your assessment."

Belle was scowling. "Hogwash," she grumbled. "Of course they'd fight, they're cranky old men! Anyway, Wilma isn't here to settle arguments. She's here to take me to the beach, the darling." She had turned all sweet again and was clutching at Willa's arm.

"It's *Willa*, and I'm sorry, I can't. I just came to —"

Belle snatched a poster from her hand and scowled as she looked it over. "Yesterday it was newspapers, today it's odd jobs. You're in every racket going!" She crumpled the poster and tossed it over her shoulder. "We've already got someone! Don't let the door hit you on the way out!" She flicked off the brake on her chair and rolled through the dining room and out into the kitchen, Baz padding along behind her. Willa turned back to the old man, Horace. He shrugged.

"Miss Trang is not fond of outsiders coming into the house, so you should probably be on your way."

He gestured kindly but firmly toward the door. Willa hung back. None of this was going the way it should. Her voice dropped to a whisper. "How many people live here?" The old man scratched his head. "People? That rather depends on your definition...."

Willa continued, the words tumbling out. "Is ... is Miss Trang ... keeping all of you prisoner here?" Horace blinked a couple of times then burst into laughter.

"Prisoner? Keeping us PRISONER? HAhahahah!" He slapped his knee and doubled over, guffawing loudly.

Willa blushed. "I just thought ... " she began, but was interrupted by a tremendous CRASH from the kitchen. Horace headed that way, still howling with laughter.

"Girls! Wait'll you hear this!"

Willa winced. How could she have been so wrong ... about *everything*? Laughter erupted in the kitchen. It was time to leave.

As she turned to go, something moved in the corner, making her jump. It was the bird, stirring in its cage. In the dim light its feathers shone dully, red and gold with a metallic sheen. Willa watched as it slowly pulled its head out from under its wing and looked at her. Willa held her breath. Instead of the parrot she thought it was, this creature looked more like a hawk or an eagle. Long, sharp talons gripped the perch, and above a cruel yellow beak two eyes burned like embers. It stared evenly at her as Willa stood frozen in her

27

tracks. As the bird looked right through her, she felt her thoughts laid out, bare and open. Then the bird blinked, and such warmth flooded into its eyes that Willa felt comforted, embraced, and happy. And strong. And brave. It was odd, but she no longer felt the sting of embarrassment over her misguided mission, even though she could still hear Horace and the ladies giggling in the kitchen.

Reluctantly, Willa turned to leave, but caught sight of something scurrying under the sofa. It must be one of the cats she kept hearing but not seeing. Willa bent to look beneath the sofa. "Here kitty, kitty ..."

There was a soft skittering and a rustling in the floor-length drapes. Willa followed the sound along the drapes to a big armchair in the corner. *Aha! Got you cornered now*, thought Willa as she knelt on the chair and looked over the high back.

Crouched on the floor behind the chair was a hairy little man, only a few inches tall, staring up at her with large, scared eyes. Willa stared in shock. Behind her an angry voice suddenly filled the room.

"WHAT IN HEAVEN'S NAME ARE YOU DOING?"

Willa spun around. Miss Trang was in the doorway, a bag of groceries in her arms, her face dark with anger. Willa shrunk back in the chair.

"I — I was just ... looking for your cat, and ..." Her voice trailed off. Horace, Belle, and Baz appeared in the dining room, watching with wide eyes.

Miss Trang dropped the bag and tin cans clattered across the floor. "We don't HAVE a cat!" she hissed, moving slowly toward Willa and casting a cold, cold shadow. Willa opened her mouth but no words came out. Miss Trang leaned closer and closer, until her face was inches from Willa's. Willa stared into her unblinking eyes — they were golden in colour, with flicks of red shooting through them. She held her breath as Miss Trang stared at her for a long, terrible moment.

Swick! Everyone turned to see a tiny suitcase slide out from under the piano, followed by the hairy little man Willa had seen behind the chair. He crawled out, his face puckered purposefully, picked up the suitcase, and stomped toward the front door.

Miss Trang's mood changed as she spun to follow the little man out into the hall. "Wait! Don't go!" she pleaded. "She didn't mean it. It won't happen again!" Belle shook her head at Willa. Horace gave her a sympathetic grimace. In the hall the front door opened and closed with a bang.

Willa peeked out the window. The little man reached the sidewalk, looked right, then left, then right again, before marching off to the right.

"Now you've done it," Belle muttered ominously. "Do you know how hard it is to find a good brownie? He worked day and night, *nonstop.* And never asked for a penny in return. Lived entirely on tea and biscuits."

Willa was stunned. "That was a *brownie?*"

Before anyone could answer her, Miss Trang re-entered the living room, ducking to fit through the doorway. Her eyes were really ablaze now. Her hair had worked its way out of her neat little bun and was floating like snakes in the air around her head.

"You interfering little pest! Why do you keep bothering us?" Her voice boomed, lower than before. And she was getting larger by the minute. Her head brushed the ceiling now, and her shoulders had broadened. The room seemed crowded, too small to hold her. As she advanced on Willa, teacups and china figurines fell crashing to the floor. Belle and Baz disappeared into the kitchen. Horace remained, trying to make peace.

"Miss Trang, please! Think of your blood pressure."

She loomed over Willa now, her head hunched forward as her shoulders pressed up against the ceiling. She became wedged there for a moment and flailed around with one arm, smashing the ceiling lamp. The room went dark. Willa dropped to the floor and crawled between Miss Trang's tree trunk legs as the woman thrashed about in the dark, breathing noisily through her nose and grunting like a great beast.

Willa reached the dim light of the hall, stumbling through the tin cans to the front door. Behind her Miss Trang, or the thing that used to be Miss Trang, roared out after her as she made her escape.

"Don't tell anyone what you saw here! I'm warning you!"

Willa didn't tell a soul. In fact, as the next few days dragged on in their boring and ordinary way, it became harder and harder to believe the incident had happened at all. Willa couldn't stop thinking about the place. It seemed every time she pondered one of the house's mysteries another five or six came to mind. First the coins, then Miss Trang, then the old man in the tree who had pelted her with acorns again as she ran away that day. And what about the loud crashing upstairs, and the strange bird, and the little man behind the armchair? Was it possible? Did brownies really exist?

And then there were the tin cans. The ones she had tripped over in the front hall. Cat food.

Chapter Three

The summer was definitely not working out as planned. Willa's odd jobs work hadn't really taken off. She spent one hot day cleaning out Mr. Santos's garage, and another afternoon washing Mrs. Blanding's St. Bernard dog, who managed to get soap suds all over her, the yard, and the neighbour's fence, which she then had to wash off as well. Other than those jobs and three lawns to mow, for the next week or so Willa didn't have much to do except think about the old folks in the boarding house. Once she had regained her nerve she began to wander by there once in a while, walking slowly, hoping to see someone but ready to run if it was Miss Trang. To her disappointment the curtains were always drawn tight and not a soul could be seen. She wondered if they'd all left town. Maybe Belle had finally gotten her way and they'd gone to the seaside for a vacation.

"Honey! You've got a job this morning! Hurry up and I'll take you on my way to work."

Her mom was rushing around the kitchen as Willa straggled down the stairs, trying to flatten her crazy slept-on hair with her hands. She was tired but glad for the work — she felt guilty she hadn't been making much money so far this summer.

Mom pushed some toast toward her with a glass of juice. "A lady just called, wants you to come by right away."

Willa spread some marmalade on her toast and grimaced. "I hope it's not another garage."

"She didn't say what she wanted you for. It's at that old place, the rooming house near the park. Now hurry and eat, I'm running late." Her mom hurried out the door, not seeing her daughter turn deathly pale.

"Miss Trang!"

During the drive Willa tried to think of a way to tell her mom, but what could she say? That she saw a tiny little man and this lady got mad and grew real big, so Willa ran away? Not a chance. The only way out was to walk up to the front door, and as soon as her mom was out of sight, get the heck out of there.

Willa got out of the car very slowly. The house looked quiet, the windows dark.

"See you later, hon," her mom called.

Willa smiled weakly as she started up the walk. She paused below the willow, glancing up, but Tengu wasn't in the tree. She looked back. Her mom was still there, waiting until she was inside. Her heart thumped as she tiptoed up the porch steps. At the front door she reached out a shaky hand but just pretended to ring the bell. She'd say there was no one at home, it was a crank phone call. Her mom was still watching as she turned, did a big shrug, and started down the steps again. Behind her the door swung open.

"Come on in, dearie. She's waiting for you."

Baz stood in the doorway, eyes narrowed and grinning slyly. Willa was trapped. She was steered inside as her mom waved and drove off.

Baz ushered her into the parlour. Willa stared in shock. It didn't look like the same room at all. Dirty plates and teacups were perched on every available flat surface, books and magazines were scattered everywhere, the plants were yellowed and droopy. Paintings hung crooked on the walls and broken glass crunched under her shoes.

"This is what happens when a brownie quits." Willa jumped, her heart in her throat. Miss Trang stood in the kitchen doorway, but she was normal size again. Her hair was neatly tucked into her bun, and though stern, she looked very ordinary.

Willa looked down at her shoes, not sure of what to say. Miss Trang continued. "But let's not talk about that, shall we? Let's get right to the reason you're here. I can't keep up with the work around here. I need help, and despite my reservations, it was suggested to me that you would be the best choice for the job." She held up a paper — one of Willa's posters.

"Will you help us out with the cleaning until we can find another brownie?"

Willa nodded dumbly. And that was how she came to work for Miss Trang.

Willa was hired to come in three times a week, arriving promptly at nine a.m. and leaving at noon. She was to clean the entire main floor — entrance, hall, parlour, dining room, and kitchen — except for Miss Trang's office, which she was not to enter. Upstairs she had to clean the hallways and the washroom, but was *not under any circumstances* to go into any of the bedrooms or the library. The backyard and stable (*Stable!* thought Willa excitedly) were expressly out of bounds. Most importantly, she was not to tell anybody *anything* about the house or its inhabitants. Miss Trang was adamant about that. "And I will *know it* if you do," she said ominously, and Willa believed her. On top of everything else the hourly wage was very generous. Willa began right away.

As she loaded stained teacups into the kitchen sink, Willa took a deep breath and tried to still her trembling hands. She couldn't believe she was actually there. For weeks she had been dying to know what was going on in this place, and now she had her own key! Willa worked very, very hard at her new job. She tidied up after the oldsters, who left things everywhere. She dusted the many, many knick-knacks — china figurines, exotic lacquer boxes, souvenir spoons from around the world, ornately carved letter-openers, framed photos with the images fading away, collections of pebbles, seashells, and pine cones. She washed legions of teacups, mopped the floors, and scrubbed the windows. And she took great care to water and care for the plants, which slowly perked up and stopped dropping their leaves.

As glad as Willa was for the work, as time went on she was not finding much satisfaction in her job. She wasn't getting any answers to her many questions, that's for sure. And she felt terribly isolated. Everyone stayed in their bedrooms while she worked. Even Miss Trang spent the entire time in her office. Willa sometimes heard her muttering to herself in there. She ran into Horace in the hall one day, and he admitted, in a whisper, that they were supposed to stay away from Willa as much as possible. Since her friends were out of town, the only people she had to talk to all day were her mom and dad, and she couldn't tell them anything at all about the house, because of her promise to Miss Trang. It was all very frustrating.

The only soul she had for company was the bird in the parlour. A small tarnished plaque on the cage read "Fadiyah." Willa began talking to her, calling her "Fadi." After all, the bird seemed to be her only friend in the house. Just taking a break and gazing into the bird's eyes for a moment or two gave Willa that warm, happy feeling she had felt the first time she'd seen her.

Days passed without event. Once she found Baz snoozing on the sofa and had to tiptoe around, cleaning quietly. A couple of times she met Belle wheeling to or from the bathroom, where she loved to take long, long baths, but the old lady always ignored her completely.

This made Willa very sad, because there was something about Belle that fascinated her. There was a deep, silent melancholy about her that just broke Willa's heart. Sometimes Willa could hear her humming up in her room. The sound made her stop what she was doing and listen, transfixed, until it faded away to silence. It was hard to believe that such haunting music could come from that cranky old dame.

In all this time she didn't catch even a glimpse of the cat that she knew *had* to be there. There were white cat hairs on the sofa, one cupboard in the kitchen was full of cat food tins, and occasionally she could swear she heard, or felt, a deep thrumming purr coming from somewhere upstairs. Yet Miss Trang had insisted that they had no cat. Why would she want to keep it a secret? Her mind reeled with this and other questions....
Why was there a padlock on the doll's house in the parlour? Why did the brownie leave? How did a bunch of old people come to be living in a house with a magic brownie? Nothing made any sense. Willa was desperate to know the full story of the house, but she wasn't about to pry or break any of the rules, because she sure didn't like it when Miss Trang got angry. No, she was determined to stay on the woman's good side from now on. Of course there was no rule against keeping her eyes and ears open, and that's what she did.

One grey and dreary day Willa was mopping the second floor hallway. One wall was lined with large windows looking out onto the back garden, and as she wrung out her mop Willa stared out at the view. She could just make out the stable, a crumbling, ivy-covered stone building at the back of the rather large property. The rest of the yard was an overgrown mess of vines, shrubs, huge oak trees, and rose bushes gone wild, so it was hard to see what else might be back there. She was just trying to picture how it might have looked in days gone by when she heard a soft tapping sound behind her.

The hallway was empty. The sound came again. She moved quietly down the hall until she reached the library door. Tap, tap. She looked up. A slender branch poked out from the top of the tall door, sporting three droopy yellow leaves. The leaves were tapping gently against the door. One of them detached and fell to the floor at her feet. She picked it up. It was dry and cracked in her hands. Willa had carefully brought all the other plants back to life, and now she desperately wanted to water this poor thing. She wasn't allowed to enter the library, but Miss Trang had gone out to buy the groceries, and it would only take a moment....

She refilled her watering can downstairs in the kitchen (since Belle was in the bathroom, as usual) and returned to the library door. She pushed it open. It was dark, there was nobody in sight, and she could see the plant in the corner right beside the door. Carefully keeping her feet planted in the hallway, she leaned in and poured water into the pot, which began to make the strangest gurgling sounds.

"Hello, Willa." She jumped. Horace was peering around the edge of a high, wing-backed chair by the window. "Come in."

Willa shook her head. "I'm not supposed to be in here. Miss Trang said. I just noticed the plant was dying...."

Horace raised an amused eyebrow. "It's quite all right. Come in. I'll take the blame if Miss Trang catches you. Besides, the hibiscus has already invited you in." He gestured to the plant. "Does it *look* like it's dying?"

She took a step into the room and looked the plant up and down. It was perfectly green, healthy, and bushy. It was sending runners out all over the room. They trailed across the tops of the bookshelves and down the sides. One little vine was even draped over Horace's chair.

"But ... the leaves that were sticking out of the door were dead."

Horace laughed and shook a finger at the plant. "Playing tricks on our new friend!" He turned back to Willa. "I think it was just curious to meet you."

"Curious? How could it be curious?"

"Come over here. Have a seat."

She gingerly walked over to join him. She sat in one of the big leather chairs, her feet dangling. Horace pulled a volume from a shelf and flipped through the pages. He showed her a diagram of the same plant. "Gossiping hibiscus. Very rare."

"Why is it called that?"

Horace smiled. "Plants have all the patience in the world. The only thing they have to worry about is growing. This one, however, listens. It knows all our secrets and one day it might just tell all!"

Willa was staring at him. "But plants can't talk."

"It called you in here, didn't it? You heard it."

He replaced the book as Willa thought about the tapping leaves. And the other odd things in the house.

"Can you tell me about the brownie?"

"What do you want to know?"

"I still don't know why he left. And is he really a brownie?"

Horace leaned on one elbow. "He certainly is. Brownies are very hard workers. That little fellow kept this whole place together. Worked day and night. Never complained and never took a day off. But brownies are also very secretive. If you *try* to see one, they pack up and leave forever." He snapped his fingers. "And you're left to wash your dishes yourself."

Willa thought this over. "When Miss Trang got so angry ..."

Horace stopped her. "Willa, surely you've noticed there are some rather ... odd things about this place. Miss Trang is very worried about people out there finding out about us. She just wants to keep outsiders out. When she became so angry with you, she wanted to scare you into staying away."

"So she wouldn't really have hurt me?"

Horace sighed. "Well, I can't say that for sure. Miss Trang is full of surprises. None of us are entirely sure what it's capable of."

"*It?*"

Horace smiled. "I meant 'she,' of course. Now maybe you'd better scoot out of here before she gets back, hmm?"

Willa nodded.

On her way back down the hall she paused at the bathroom door. Belle loved her two- and three-hour baths, but it sure was a pain to mop up all the water she left on the floor. Willa had no idea how Belle managed to climb from the tub into her wheelchair on her own. She tapped gently on the door.

"Belle? Are you going to be much longer? I need to clean in there." No answer. "Do you need any help? Belle?" She put her ear to the door and to her horror heard a faint gurgling sound. Dropping the watering can she jerked the door open, but it caught on the chain. Through the crack she saw Belle sit up in the tub with a splash, hissing at her angrily: "GET OUT!!"

"Sorry!" Willa quickly retreated. She leaned against the closed door for a moment and shut her eyes. The scene flashed through her mind ... the silvery hair, the shiny white skin ... the green scales, the fins.

Belle was a mermaid.

Chapter Four

A weekend of worries and a very, very strange dinner

Willa finished up her work in the kitchen, trembling and anxious. Above her she heard Belle roll out of the bathroom and down the hall into her room, slamming the door behind her. Willa left for home soon after, ducking out before Miss Trang came home. It was Friday, so she had all weekend to fret and worry. Would Belle tell on her? Willa figured the fact that Belle was a mermaid would be pretty high on the list of things Miss Trang didn't want her to know about. She shivered every time she thought about Miss Trang getting angry. And every time she shut her eyes she saw the glimmering scales. At least now she knew why Belle wanted so badly to go to the ocean.

The weekend crawled by. There was no distraction from her worries until Sunday night, when Grandpa came over for dinner.

"Willa the Whisp!" he cackled as she ran up to give him a big hug. His ratty old sweater smelled of pipe smoke and salt air. His sunbeaten face was set in a perpetual grin, and his white hair stuck out in all directions, like he'd just come in from a gale. Willa always teased him about his hair. She even put a comb in his Christmas stocking one year, but he'd just laughed and played a tune on it with tissue paper.

Over dinner Grandpa entertained them with his favourite topics: the weather, the sea, and the weather out on the sea. Willa even forgot about Belle for a few minutes, listening happily.

Grandpa was loud and full of life. She could just picture him out on the water in his little boat, waving and calling out to the other boats. She knew his bad luck had made him infamous among the other fishermen. They all had good years and bad years, but Grandpa hadn't caught a single fish for as long as Willa had been alive, and even before. Whenever his boat wasn't rented out he'd still go out on the ocean, but not to fish. He claimed his trips were "picnic pleasure cruises," but Willa knew he still had nets and rods stowed away on the boat, all carefully maintained and at the ready. Once he'd told her some of the other fishermen wouldn't even talk to him, they thought he was bad luck. Willa had been outraged, but he'd just laughed. "Superstitious old fools!"

Now, as Grandpa paused to shovel down his vegetables, Willa stared down at her peas and carrots and thought about the ocean. In her mind she saw Belle, slipping out of her wheelchair and sinking down into the sea, her silvery hair floating on the water and her tail flicking shimmery droplets into the air.

She cornered him after supper while her parents cleared the table.

"Grandpa ... there are a lot of ... strange things living in the ocean, right?"

"You bet."

"Things that seem ... magic, even?"

He looked at her curiously. "Spit it out. What do you want to know?"

"Have you ever seen a mermaid?" She was afraid he'd laugh at her, but instead he started, his eyes wide with surprise.

"Well, now. What an odd question."

"I was just ... I'm reading a book about them," she fibbed. At this he relaxed, his face falling into the smile she'd been expecting in the first place.

"You want to know if there is magic out there in the world. Well ... *that* depends on who is doing the looking." And that's all he would say on the matter.

She was still thinking about his words when she went up to bed. She found a small white card on her pillow and smiled, thinking it was from him. It wasn't. It was not signed, but Willa knew in the pit of her stomach that the long, spidery handwriting had to be Miss Trang's. The card read:

> *It is not necessary for you to come in to work tomorrow morning, but you are cordially invited to join us for dinner tomorrow night. 6 p.m. Do not be late.*

How did the card get there? Was Miss Trang angry? Belle must have told. What was going to happen? At best she would probably lose her job. And at worst? She had no way of knowing. Even Horace said he didn't know what Miss Trang was capable of. And yet she had to go to the dinner. If she didn't, she knew she would never be able to go back, and the thought of all her questions about the house going unanswered forever was enough to drive her up the wall.

And so the next evening she walked up to the front door of the boarding house at exactly six o'clock, knees shaking, hands trembling, and brain rattling. Baz swung the door open. She didn't say a word, simply waved Willa into the parlour.

The lights were so low she could barely see. Miss Trang stood in the centre of the room and seated around her were Belle, Horace, Baz, and another gentleman in an armchair in the darkest corner — she could barely make him out at all. Miss Trang stepped forward, her eyes glittering in the gloom.

"Willa, we have invited you here tonight for a reason. You know ... about Belle." She raised an eyebrow and Willa nodded. "A very serious matter. We held a house meeting to discuss what was to be done about you." A shiver ran down Willa's spine. Miss Trang looked her straight in the eye.

"Willa Fuller. Would you like to continue working here?"

Willa nodded quickly.

Miss Trang regarded her for a moment before going

on. "This house is exactly what it appears to be. An ordinary retirement home for seniors. The only part that isn't so ordinary is that we have retired from, shall we say, rather *unusual* careers in ... a different world from yours. A different time."

The others were all nodding.

Miss Trang pursed her lips thoughtfully. "You might be someone useful to us, someone from the outside we can trust. Someone of uncommon character. "

Someone useful? What did they want her to do? Willa wondered wildly. And did she have uncommon character? She didn't think so. Miss Trang was looking her up and down as if she was thinking the same thing.

"We need to know whether you can handle the rather *odd* things in this house without losing your *nerve.*"

Willa didn't know what to say, so she just nodded.

Miss Trang continued. "Tonight's dinner will be your test. You will finally meet all the residents of this house and see them as they really are. You will have dinner with us and ask no questions. You will be on your best behaviour and not stare, understand?"

"Yes, ma'am." How hard could that be? Just be polite, keep quiet, and eat. Still, butterflies were fluttering in her stomach and she felt short of breath.

"Fine," said Miss Trang. "Let's begin. You already know Mirabel." Belle rolled forward in her chair and pulled the blanket off her shiny, shimmery mermaid tail. Willa glanced at it for only a moment then locked onto Belle's cool eyes. She curtsied. Belle raised an eyebrow and nodded quickly.

46

"Baz." Baz stepped forward, smiling, but looking her old self. No surprises there. "Tengu." She hadn't even seen the little man from the willow tree where he stood beside the piano. Now he stepped up, bowing to her, then adopting a fighting posture.

"Perhaps a display of my terrifying skills of combat—" He drew an elbow back sharply, knocking the birdcage behind him. Fadi hissed and gave him the evil eye. Miss Trang just shook her head wearily.

"No, no. Nothing of that sort is required, thank you." Tengu gave a little karate chop in the air and stepped back, grinning at Willa.

Miss Trang gestured toward Horace. "Professor Horace St. Smithenwick."

The old gentleman stepped forward and bowed very slowly. At least it looked like he was bowing, but he just kept leaning down and down until his fingers touched the floor, and as soon as they touched, his whole body began to change. Willa stared as his tweed jacket rippled smoothly into golden fur. His fingers curled on the carpet into paws and a long tail suddenly flicked in the air. He had transformed into a lion! Not all of him, though — his head was the same as before, the wavy silver hair, the kind eyes and the wire-rimmed glasses. Trembling, Willa stood her ground as the Horace-lion padded right up to her. She looked straight into his eyes, trying to forget the terrible long claws at the ends of his paws. Horace circled her, his tail tickling her shoulders and making her shiver. She took a deep breath to calm herself as he made his way into the dining room.

"You haven't yet met Robert." Miss Trang nodded to the corner where the man in the armchair sat. In the gloom Willa could just make out glittering black eyes, a rather large red nose, and wisps of white hair combed across a very bald head. He wore a cardigan sweater over a rumpled shirt and tie. A very ordinary-looking old man, until the armchair beneath him rose unsteadily to stand on its four long legs. It wasn't an armchair at all, it was his body, a horse's body — four legs with hooves. He was a centaur. Willa had seen pictures of them in books, but they were always young. She'd never seen a picture of an old man centaur. His head was slightly bowed as it brushed the ceiling. His hooves thudded on the thick carpet as he moved slowly and carefully past her into the dining room, but he still managed to knock over a couple of chairs as he went.

Willa's heart was thumping. It was all too terribly exciting, but she was working to remain calm and composed. Or at least to look like she was.

"And last but not least, Mab."

Willa looked around but no one was left. Everyone had gone into the dining room. Miss Trang pulled a small key from her pocket and went over to the dollhouse. She unlocked the padlock and opened up the front of the house, revealing tiny, perfect furnished rooms inside. In one room a small doll, no bigger than her little finger, sat on the sofa in a beautiful shimmery dress.

"Come on now," Miss Trang murmured. "It's all right." Willa gasped in surprise as the "doll" stood up.

48

"Pleased to meet you," sounded a faint, insect-buzzy voice.

Willa was so gobsmacked she couldn't speak for a moment. "Pleased to meet you," she finally stammered.

Mab walked to the edge of her little room and jumped into the air. Sparkly transparent wings carried her flitting out of the room and into the dining room.

A fairy! A real live fairy! Willa felt her heart would burst. When she was very little she had spent countless hours in the backyard searching under toadstools and behind leaves for fairies. The pursuit eventually felt too silly and childish and she had turned to other pastimes, like stamp collecting. And now here she was, and fairies were real after all! She was so delighted and excited she wanted to laugh out loud. She had a million questions, but of course it was all a test, and if she failed she would never, ever see darling little Mab again, or Belle, or any of them, so she kept her mouth shut.

Miss Trang ushered Willa into the dining room. Everyone took their places around the table and Willa realized suddenly that she was quite hungry. She'd been so nervous about coming that she'd barely eaten a bite all day.

"Dinner smells delicious," she ventured, which was true. Now the smells from the kitchen — pot roast with gravy, it smelled like — were making her mouth water. Baz hurried in and out, filling the table with covered dishes. When she was done, Miss Trang stood and, with a flourish, whipped the cover from a large silver soup tureen.

"Oooh!" and "Aah!" and "Lovely!" were heard around the table but all Willa could do was stare. The tureen was totally empty. She looked around to see if it was a joke, but everyone was dead serious. They held up their bowls and Miss Trang made a great show of ladling out nothing but air.

"Willa, would you like some soup?" All faces turned toward her. She froze. She had no idea what she was supposed to do. Was it special magic invisible food that everyone could see but her? Or was it a big joke? Were they laughing at her?

Willa smiled weakly and held up her bowl. "Yes, please. I'd love some soup."

Everyone seemed to relax at that and began chatting over their imaginary meals. To Willa's right Robert jostled her elbow as he leaned forward to slurp up his nonexistent soup. Horace too lowered his face right into his bowl, lapping noisily. The others wielded their silver spoons, clattering them in the bowls and delicately lifting them to their mouths.

Over the main course Robert began arguing loudly with Baz about the amount of garlic in the non-existent mashed potatoes. He occasionally pounded a hoof on the floor for emphasis, shaking the whole table. Horace listened to them, chewing thoughtfully. His massive paws rested on the table, the claws idly tapping holes in the tablecloth.

Willa sat primly, quietly, trying not to stare. Right beside her sparkling little Mab was skipping about her plate as if it was a fairy ring, the china sounding ting-ting-ting with every step. And Baz kept creeping up silently behind Willa, making her jump every time she placed a new empty plate in front of her.

The only thing that kept Willa from getting jittery was Fadi in her cage, just visible over Belle's shoulder. The bird watched her steadily but kindly and even winked at her once. All she could do was pretend to eat. After all, that's what everyone else was doing.

Willa dabbed her mouth with her napkin and placed it on her plate. The so-called meal was finally over. Now she had to pretend she was full, even though her stomach was groaning. Suddenly something brushed against her ankle. She stiffened. What new weird creature could this be? Was it dangerous? It was circling her feet, she could feel it moving. It must be the cat, the mysterious cat she had never seen. She picked up her handkerchief and let it slip from her hand onto the floor. Nobody even looked up as she leaned down to retrieve it and peered into the darkness under the table. Two green eyes peered back, and a scaly lizard face flicked out a scarlet tongue at her.

She managed not to scream but jerked up suddenly, banging her head on the table. Sitting up as nonchalantly as possible, she quietly drew up her legs until she was sitting cross-legged on her chair. She realized she was holding her breath and let it out slowly and silently. This was too much all at once; she felt an urge to shout, or run or scream or SOMETHING, but she kept rigidly still.

Everything had become strangely quiet. Everyone at the table was watching her, smiling.

"How did you like your dinner?" Miss Trang was regarding her with transparent eyes.

"It was delicious, thank you very much." All she could think about was getting out of there and going home to make herself a peanut butter sandwich.

"This was all Horace's idea." said Miss Trang, gesturing toward the empty plates.

Horace nodded, grinning. "It's known as a Barmecide Feast — a test of poise and humour. You did very well indeed, my dear."

Willa blinked, unsure of what to say. Her stomach spoke for her, gurgling loudly, and she blushed with embarrassment. Miss Trang turned to Baz.

"Go and make Willa a sandwich. Peanut butter, yes?"

Willa started in surprise and nodded. Baz scurried into the kitchen and in a flash returned with the sandwich. As Willa munched happily, Miss Trang spoke once more.

"Since you have done so well tonight, we'd like to keep you on as our housekeeper. You'll have additional duties, so we'll need you here full time. And there are two rules. The first rule you know already: do not tell *anyone* about *anything* that goes on here. The second concerns the asking of questions. I'm sure you have a few queries about our humble household, yes?"

Willa could only nod, as her mouth was full.

"Well, it would take many days and nights to explain everything you are wondering about, believe me. For this reason you are only allowed one question per day."

Willa swallowed. "May I ask one now?" Miss Trang nodded but Tengu was already pointing at Willa and cackling.

"That was a question! You used up your question!"

Miss Trang gave him a stern look and he sat back, one hand over his mouth as he continued to snicker. "Go ahead." She nodded to Willa.

Willa's mind raced. What did she most want to know about? The fairy? The bird Fadiyah? Horace the lion? Robert the centaur?

Hearing the sudden tick-tick-tick of nails on the wood floor, Willa peered back over her shoulder to see the long, skinny lizard dash across the room, jumping, writhing, and wriggling. She thought it was biting at its own tail, but soon saw that it had two heads, one at either end, which snapped at each other with jagged teeth! Finally one clamped onto the neck of the other. The lizard formed a hoop and rolled away out of sight. Willa turned back to Miss Trang.

"Don't you own a cat?" she asked. The table erupted into guffaws and squeals of laughter. The bird squawked. Even Miss Trang smiled.

"The answer to that is no."

Which was all very well, but when Willa arrived for work the next morning there was a dead little bird waiting for her on the doorstep, looking for all the world like a cat's welcome gift.

Chapter Five

Willa returned to work, doing the same chores plus new ones, since she now had to clean and tidy the entire house. She didn't mind in the least. The extra pay of a real *full*-time job made her parents very proud. The mood at home became much more relaxed, which was great. No more talk about "money worries."

Willa's days at the boarding house changed from quiet to boisterous. Everyone could now go about as they pleased while Willa was there. They bickered in the parlour, pestered Baz for tea and biscuits, and generally got underfoot as Willa was trying to clean. Robert awkwardly clip-clopped through the too-small rooms, knocking things over with his tail. Being so restricted in space made him extremely cross and argumentative, though he was always civil to Willa. And Horace was very kind to her too. He was usually in his human form, although once in a while she'd chance upon him as a lion, curled up on the carpet for a nap, and taking up the entire room. Mab occasionally flitted by her, glittering and giggly. Tengu grinned when he saw Willa and did his best to talk her into a friendly arm wrestle or some other contest of strength. She always declined, though, fearing that she might win. Baz was friendly enough, even though Willa always felt she was snickering at her.

Belle, however, was another story entirely. She rolled through the house, pushed by Baz or wheeling herself, with nothing but a scowl and a hrrmph for Willa, who had no idea what she'd done to incur the old lady's wrath. Belle seemed to blame her for some ancient injustice. Maybe she just didn't like kids. Or maybe she hated everyone from the "outside." Whatever the reason, the mermaid was always in a foul mood and Willa tried to stay out of her way.

The old folks spent their days sniping at each other, not always good-naturedly, while the bird clucked disapprovingly in the corner. Squabbles quieted immediately whenever Miss Trang emerged from her office, gliding quiet and mysterious through the house, but resumed as soon as she was out of earshot.

Despite all distractions, Willa spent her days diligently focussed on her work. The cleaning of the upstairs bedrooms was no small job, as the old folk were all packrats and had been accumulating possessions for *hundreds* of years. The dark and dusty rooms were full, floor-to-ceiling full, of weird odds and ends. Horace's room was crowded with a huge collection of bird feathers, mounted and framed, or simply stuck into jars, vases, books. His books too were overwhelming, tottering stacks of them everywhere. Some had pages so faded they were totally illegible, while others were in languages Horace admitted he had no knowledge of. And yet he refused to let Willa dispose of any of them, even the ones which were entirely missing their pages, eaten out by bugs or some other long-gone pest.

"What if they fell into the wrong hands?" He'd throw his hands up in despair at the thought.

"Whatever hands they fell into would just throw them in the trash!" countered Willa, but Horace just smiled.

Robert didn't keep so many things, but his room had its own challenges. To accomodate his height, a hole had been broken in the ceiling so that his room opened into the attic, which was teeming with spiders, and sometimes bats as well. (Willa never saw any sign of mice, however. If there wasn't an actual cat on the premises keeping them out, she felt there must surely be some kind of *ghost* cat at work.) Robert didn't seem to mind insects or pests, but they made it doubly hard for Willa to keep the place even remotely tidy.

Tengu's room, on the other hand, was a snap to clean. It was a small room, simple and clutter-free. He slept on a mat on the floor and had next to no personal possessions. That's not to say he didn't *want* things, though. Willa often heard him begging Miss Trang for ...

"A bardiche? Or a morningstar! No? How about a sweet little shuriken? Just one?"

Willa would go to the immense dictionary in the library to look up his requests — massive medieval weapons mostly, pretty gruesome-looking. And the "sweet little shuriken" was a razor-sharp throwing star. Fortunately

Miss Trang held firm. No weapons was a fundamental house rule. *Thank goodness for that*, thought Willa.

Baz's room was dominated by a great huge cabinet with dozens of tiny drawers containing all sorts of dried herbs, dead bugs, and reptiles, and unidentifiable bits of fuzz which made Willa queasy. Belle had a wardrobe full of gorgeous clothes she never wore and an ornate vanity table with a beautiful set of ivory and pearl brushes and combs. A golden inlaid with gemstones probably held her jewellery, though Willa didn't have the nerve to peek inside. Mab's dollhouse was usually tidy enough, which was good, because Willa didn't know how she'd ever dust in there without breaking something. Miss Trang's room was the only one she was still not allowed to enter, though she could now go in to clean the office.

Baz did all the cooking, but Willa helped there too whenever she could. The backyard remained off limits to her. Willa thought it would be wonderful if it was cut back, mowed, and cleaned up. As Miss Trang pointed out, however, the overgrown trees and bushes effectively shielded them from the prying eyes of the outside world — most notably the nosy next-door neighbours, Mr. and Mrs. Hackett. The Hacketts were fond of calling to Willa from their front porch, waving her over as she was arriving or leaving so they could complain about something ... most often the abysmal condition of the front or back yards. They were annoyed enough at the sight of a single weed in a neighbouring lawn, so naturally the jungle in Miss Trang's backyard was really driving them up the wall. It was part of Willa's job to listen sympathetically and try to keep on good terms with the Hacketts, which was possibly the hardest part of her work at the house.

There was a lot to do, but Willa arrived every morning eager and excited. She worked hard to finish her chores as quickly as possible so she'd have at least some of the afternoon free, all the while pondering what question she would ask that day. It was a difficult decision to make. Willa felt fortunate to be in Miss Trang's good graces at last, so she certainly didn't want to push her luck by being too inquisitive. And she was still a little afraid of Miss Trang, so she decided to steer clear of her for the first week at least. Better to start with the others, and the simpler, more straightforward questions.

So on her very first day she sought out Horace, in the library as usual, and in human form. The day outside was rainy and grey, and the library was dark, but there was a fire lit in the fireplace and the chairs were big and cozy. Horace smiled to see her and set his book aside.

"Come. Sit down." Willa climbed into a tall wingback chair as he poured her some tea. He passed the cup and looked at her kindly. "You'd like to ask me something?"

"Yes, please. If you don't mind. I was wondering what you ... what exactly ..." She paused awkwardly.

"What exactly am I?" Willa nodded and sipped her tea. Horace sighed, removing his glasses and rubbing his eyes. Then he stood and walked to the centre of the hearth rug. He began to pace in deliberate circles, the way cats do before they lie down. On the first round he glowed golden in the dancing light of the fire.

58

On the second round he dropped onto all fours and hair streamed around his face. On the third round the golden fur flowed down his neck and back until he had turned once more into a lion and lay down on the rug, yawning contentedly.

Willa stared. The change had been so smooth, so ... normal. Now Horace lay there, his forepaws extended before him. His face was the only thing that remained the same. It was still a human, Horace face, but fringed with a golden lion's mane. When he spoke his voice was even more velvety, as if he might fall into purring at any moment.

"I am an Androsphinx, from the ancient time of the pharoahs in Egypt." Willa listened breathlessly as Horace explained how very, very old he was. He explained how some sphinxes were warlike and enjoyed eating human flesh ... as he said this his nose crinkled in distaste, and he hastened to assure Willa that he was a more peaceable sort than that.

"Besides, humans are just ... not very tasty, no matter how you prepare them," he sniffed. Willa sank further into her chair, very thankful for this fact.

As the afternoon wore on and the room grew darker, rain tapped on the roof and the windows rattled, the hibiscus plant curled around their chairs, and Willa listened to Horace's tales of Egypt. She listened to his soft voice until her eyes grew heavy and it seemed that his yellow fur had turned into the very sand dunes of the desert, and the gusts of wind at the windows were whispering djinn, the evil spirits that whirl about the desert plains.

When she woke the fire had gone out in the grate, and Horace was nowhere to be seen. It all seemed like a dream, but then everything that happened in this house seemed like a dream and Willa knew that every day she spent there would be more fantastic than the last. And she was absolutely right.

The next day, after a morning of dusting so vigorously she sneezed about a hundred times, Willa had tea with little Mab, who clutched her tea-thimble with both hands as if it were a bucket. *I'm having tea with a real fairy*, Willa kept saying to herself in disbelief, though Mab wasn't quite as lovely and delicate as Willa expected fairies to be. She looked sweet enough and had a smile that made Willa want to coo over her like a baby, but whenever Mab was irritated there would be a sharp flash in her eyes and her dear smile would twist ever so slightly into a kind of gargoyle grimace which made Willa shiver.

Mab delighted in saying nasty things about the other inhabitants of the house. It always surprised Willa how much the old folks argued and fought, though she suspected it was due more to boredom than to actual hatred. Mab boasted about the tricks she played on her housemates, such as sewing their pockets shut with invisible thread, sprinkling sawdust in their lemonade, and hovering around their ears like a persistent mosquito, whispering an endless stream of insults. Mab's knowledge of rude words was extensive, covering all the ones that Willa wasn't allowed to use at home, and many more that Willa had never heard before, but which certainly sounded like words she wouldn't be allowed to use at home. Mab's main complaint was that the others didn't take her seriously, treating her like a silly little kid or referring to her as an "insect." When Mab recounted how they teased her, she'd become extremely agitated. Her language would turn a few shades more colourful, and she'd pound her little fists on the table so hard that her fine yellow hair would jump out of its silky ringlets and poke straight out on all sides, so that she looked like a dandelion, the kind that you blow on to watch the seeds fly away.

One morning the Hacketts were up in arms about being woken at an ungodly hour by an awful, ear-splitting noise coming from Miss Trang's roof. Willa promised she'd get to the bottom of it. She feared it was the bird Fadi, but Tengu gleefully claimed responsibility.

"You see," he hopped up and down in his excitement, "I've taken on the job of scaring away basilisks."

"Basilisks?" Willa looked at him questioningly.

"You don't know what basilisks are?! Really, what passes for education in your world! Basilisks are half-snake and half-rooster. They can kill you just by looking at you!" At this point he jumped at Willa, grimacing with his fingers curled like claws. Tengu was always trying to give her a scare, but it just made Willa want to laugh because the tender-hearted fellow was easily the least scary person in the entire household.

"Basilisks are repelled by the sound of a rooster crowing. But we don't have a rooster. So I get up every morning, go up on the roof, and cock-a-doodle-doo!" He snapped his fingers proudly. "So simple it's genius."

Then he did his rooster impersonation for Willa, right there in the parlour, setting the teacups rattling and the chandelier tinkling. The ruckus brought Belle rolling in and an argument began at once.

"Must you do that in the house, you *fool?*"

Willa got Tengu to agree to do his crowing a couple hours after dawn, and on the peak of the roof furthest from the Hacketts. Belle was still shaking her head.

"That sorry excuse for rooster crowing would never fool a basilisk. Never in a million years."

Tengu drew himself up to his full, unremarkable height. "I don't see any around here, do you? Therefore it *must* work!"

Then he stuck his tongue out at Belle and waggled his fingers around his ears. That started Belle hurling things at him — sofa cushions, books, shoes — until Willa begged her to stop.

Belle was easily the most unfriendly person in the house, but no matter how unpleasant she was, how cranky, how downright rude, Willa felt drawn to her. She still remembered how beautiful Belle had looked when she'd first met her, when Belle was asking to go to the seaside. That loveliness and charm could be flicked on or off like a light switch, and apparently Belle had decided Willa was to be left in the dark. Their encounters usually went something like this:

"Good morning, Belle!"

Scowl.

"And how are you today?"

Abrupt exit from room, with a dismissive toss of silver hair. Really, it was like trying to be friends with a rock.

Besides giving Miss Trang a wide berth, and trying not to antagonize Belle, Willa also tended to avoid Robert. He usually stayed in his room, but when he ventured out, knocking into the overhead lamps and smashing things with every step, Willa felt small and foolish next to him. And he always looked a little wild-eyed. The wisps of hair around his ears stuck out every which way, there were always spills and stains on his clothes, and he smelled funny. When speaking of Robert, Mab tipped her head back with her thumb pointing to her mouth, meaning he drank too much.

One day Robert and Belle happened to be in the parlour as Mab led Willa in to show her one of her special treasures. She opened up a trunk to reveal a real pearl from an oyster. Mab glowed proudly as Willa admired it. She wasn't exactly sure what Mab might do with it, since it was far too big for jewellery. Willa was just imagining the little fairy using it as a bowling ball when Robert suddenly swayed to his feet and stomped one hoof in irritation.

"A pearl. Big deal. I've got something far more valuable than that." He turned to Willa, smiling eagerly. "Would you like to see it?"

Willa nodded, a little uncertain. Robert reached for an old cigar box on the mantel.

Belle snorted. "Oh for God's sake, Robert. Not that filthy old thing."

"It's *gross*," squeaked Mab in agreement.

Robert spun around, upsetting an end table. "You two wouldn't know magic if it came up and bit you on the ass!"

He turned back to Willa, tipping over a vase, which Willa managed to catch, but not before it spilled water and daisies all over the carpet. Robert paid no mind, tapping the top of the cigar box.

"This is my good luck charm. It's the best luck charm there is, better than a rabbit's foot or a horseshoe, and it beats a four-leaf clover all to hell."

Now Willa was curious, so she leaned in as he removed the rubber band keeping the lid in place. He carefully lifted the lid to reveal what looked like a misshapen turnip.

"Oh, that's ... nice...." Willa smiled politely.

Robert beamed proudly, as if he was showing off a newborn baby. "It's a mandrake!" Seeing Willa's blank look, he went on. "The mandrake only grows at the foot of a gallows, and as you can see, the root is in the shape of a man."

Willa looked closer. The thing did have two offshoots that could be taken for arms and another two that could be legs, but it was far from obvious. She looked up to see Robert nodding and smiling, his eyes wide with delight. He looked like a little boy at show and tell.

"When the mandrake is pulled from the ground, the root screams so horribly that anyone within earshot goes instantly mad," he informed her gleefully.

"So that's what happened to you, you old goat," cackled Belle.

Willa stifled a smile as Robert let fly with a few choice words. Mab was up on the dollhouse roof, rolling around amid peals of tinkly bell laughter, while Belle rocked back and forth in her chair, grinning merrily. Willa hadn't seen Belle smile in a long, long while.

Robert grew rather huffy and returned his cigar box to the mantel. Willa tried to cheer him up, saying it was really quite fascinating and she'd never heard about mandrakes before, but he was officially in a sulk and went stomping up to his room. Willa wondered if she should go up to apologize but felt Mab tugging at her sleeve.

"I've got something else to show you. Something very, very important," her little voice chimed. Willa smiled, reminded of little children trying to top each other with their toys. She knelt on the carpet as Mab flew into the little house again. Inside, the fairy reached under a miniature armchair and pulled out a tiny sewing basket.

Willa looked over at Belle, who rolled her eyes. Mab opened the basket and carefully lifted out her knitting needles. Hanging from them was a long, silvery scarf. Willa had often seen Mab sit in that chair, clicking away with her knitting needles, but she had never before gotten a look at what the fairy was knitting. Mab lovingly draped the scarf across her arms and stroked it.

"This," she whispered, "is the most valuable treasure in the entire house." She held it out and Willa reached to touch it. The stitches were tiny and fine, and the scarf felt silky, even silkier than silk. It was like dipping her

65

finger in cool water. Suddenly Belle's mocking voice burst out behind her.

"What makes it so valuable? What's it made of, caterpillar fuzz? Moooonbeams? Magical silvery fairy farts?" Belle burst into laughter as Mab shot her a dirty look and whisked the scarf back into the basket. Willa watched helplessly as the fairy flew up and grabbed hold of the front of the dollhouse. With a last indignant "Hmph!" she slammed it shut with herself inside.

"Belle!" Willa felt bad for Mab but couldn't help but smile herself. Belle was still chuckling in amusement. Willa sat down beside her, conscious of how rare this friendly moment was. "What about you? Don't you have something special like that? Something that means the world to you?"

Belle raised her eyebrows at Willa's tone but blinked thoughtfully. Willa noticed her hand slip into a small pocket in her sweater.

"Me? Well, I ..." Belle saw Willa looking at her pocket and blushed. "It's nothing much. Just something that ... someone ... gave to me."

Willa watched closely as Belle pulled out her hand and uncurled her fingers. In her lined and wrinkled palm was a round, smooth, white stone.

"Is it magic?" Willa whispered.

Belle shook her head. "Not in the way you might think." She rolled the stone over and over in her hand. "This was given to me a long time ago. When I lived in the ocean." Her face softened into a smile at the memory, and she ran her fingers over its surface.

"Belle," ventured Willa, "why do you live here? Instead of in the ocean, I mean?" For a moment Willa was afraid she'd gone too far, but Belle just lowered her head sadly.

"I made a mistake." She tapped her breastbone with one bony finger. "I can't breathe water anymore, I can never go back. Sometimes ... I forget that." Her eyes fell on the stone again. "And this ... *this* was the start of all my troubles." She snapped it up in her hand and thrust it into her pocket. Then she seemed to suddenly remember who she was talking to and squinted angrily at Willa.

"But of course, *you* know all about it already, don't you? *Don't you?*" she hissed at Willa, making her jump. "No, I don't! I don't know what you mean!" Willa protested, shrinking back from her.

Angry as she was, there was a tear in Belle's eye as she gripped the wheels of her chair and rolled out of the room. Willa was left behind, alone and utterly confused.

Chapter Six

In which dark clouds descend and Miss Trang departs
on a mysterious journey

Belle retreated even more from Willa after that, slipping into melancholy. Willa felt the mood of the entire household change as well. The usually purposeful and efficient Miss Trang wandered aimlessly, frowning and lost in thought. As a result the others were uncommonly quiet, watching her and keeping their thoughts to themselves. It felt like everyone was waiting for something. When Willa could stand it no longer she sought out Horace in the library.

"Horace, what's going on?"

He looked up from his book. For a moment he looked so blank she thought he didn't know who she was. Then he blinked and smiled. "Ah, Willa. What's going on where?"

"Here. Everyone's acting weird. Like you're all waiting for something to happen."

Horace leaned back in his chair and rubbed his forehead. "We are, I suppose. Things just don't ... feel right. Something's wrong but we're not sure what it is. I suspect that old enemies are waking up, somewhere in the world."

"Enemies? Whose enemies?" Willa felt cold. She worried for a moment that Horace might refuse to answer more questions than the "one a day" she'd been allotted, but he kept going, smiling sadly.

"When you deal in magic and live for hundreds or thousands of years, as we have, it's quite easy to make a few enemies along the way. And they have long lives too, and long memories ... as long as time itself."

"But where are they? Are they nearby? What's happening?" The questions poured out.

"We haven't received any direct news of anything yet. Nothing has even happened that we're sure of. But there's a ... a kind of heaviness in the air. The taste of iron." He looked at her kindly. "You know when you can feel a rainstorm coming, just from the stillness?" Willa nodded. "Well, there's a feeling like that about."

He stared out the window. "It's in the air, and the light ... my very blood slows in my veins. Thickens. Everything is tensing up for something. Something's coming."

Willa looked out at the sleepy street. It was hot and still. Cicadas buzzed in the trees. Fear flooded through her. Questions froze in her throat.

Horace smiled reassuringly. "Oh, I'm being overly dramatic. Maybe nothing will happen. Old people worry too much. We've got nothing better to do." He spoke lightly but Willa was still alarmed.

"But what can you do? To find out for sure?"

"Other than wait? Well, I might try some old-fashioned augury. It's been such a long while, I'm not sure I'm still up to it ..."

"What's augury?"

Horace puffed himself up proudly. "Augury, dear Willa, is my personal specialty. It was my job in the old days to interpret the will of the gods, to tell if they were pleased or displeased with the doings of man. It was my job to foretell the future from the clues I saw around me." Then he sighed and sagged a little. "Only I'm not sure I can still do it ... I can't get a good view of things here in town."

He looked her in the eye. "Willa, there's nothing to be afraid of. Don't worry." He tucked a book under his arm and drifted toward the door. Willa squeaked out one last question before he disappeared.

"Horace ... you will tell me when there *is* something to be afraid of, won't you?"

He paused, a dark shape in the doorway. Without a word, he nodded and was gone.

For the next few days Willa tried not to worry, but everyone grew more and more sullen. Nobody spoke, not even to argue, complain, or tease. They paced or sat in the parlour staring as their tea grew cold. Willa tiptoed about and spoke only when absolutely necessary, in a hushed whisper.

One day Miss Trang's office door was ajar and Willa saw her leaning back in her chair with a cold compress over her eyes, muttering to herself.

"It's coming ... It's coming all right ... Who will it be this time?... Who?"

One night at home, a week after her conversation with Horace, Willa had an intensely vivid dream. A tornado dropped suddenly from a blue sky and roared around the boarding house, ripping off the roof and sucking all its contents up into the sky amid shrieks and wails.

Willa awoke damp with sweat. Everything was still. The room was stuffy and hot. She got up to open her window.

Orange street lamps lit the empty street. Willa pushed the window open. There was no breeze. She was wishing she had a fan in her room when the streetlamps suddenly went dark. Willa jumped. There was no moon, the street was black, and the air heavy. It was hard to breathe. She gripped the window ledge and stared at the street lamps, wishing with all her might that they'd come on again. Then she heard it. Horse hooves. Distant but growing louder every moment.

Willa listened. She wanted to step back from the window but she couldn't move, she couldn't unclench her fingers, she couldn't even breathe. The only thing still functioning was her brain, which screamed at her to move away from the window.

The hooves grew louder and louder. Willa stared up the street, petrified at what might appear. Suddenly, in the blackness, an even darker form appeared in the distance, approaching swiftly. It was a horse, an inky black horse running upright on its two hind legs, like a human. The sound of its hooves grew so loud she thought the whole neighbourhood would wake. If only it would! She didn't want to be the only person to see this.

The horse moved closer, running on two legs with such speed that its mane and tail streamed out behind. As it passed her Willa felt the hot breeze of its wake. Just past her house the horse stopped dead, not even slowing first, but instantly freezing in its tracks. Willa's heart almost jumped out of her chest. The street was silent once more as the horse turned its head from one side to the other, then, with a measured clop ... clop ... it turned and looked straight at Willa with burning red eyes.

After a long, silent moment the horse turned away ... clop ... clop ... and began to run again, disappearing quickly up the street. Willa's knees buckled and she fell to the floor.

Willa woke at dawn, still crumpled beneath the window. She felt groggy, but when the memory of the black horse shot through her brain she was suddenly wide awake. Her body ached and she longed to climb back into bed, but Willa was certain that this was what Miss Trang had been waiting for. This was what they were all waiting for. She had to go to them.

Tiptoeing out of the house, she was again gripped by fear, but the day was reassuringly normal, the rising sun warm and friendly. The paperboy was working his way up the block; she could hear the monotonous thud as each newspaper hit its front door. Everything looked so ... ordinary.

She ran all the way. The air was fresh and cool for the first time in weeks. Birds sang. The town seemed so bright and cheery, she almost doubted what she'd seen.

The house was alive with loud voices and movement. Everyone but Miss Trang was in the parlour. They were wearing their pajamas and robes, and all talking at once.

"— absolute crap!" Belle was shouting as Willa ran in.

Horace began patiently. "The signs all point to a disturbance ..."

Belle interrupted him. "A disturbance! Well, thank you, Nostradamus! We all woke up, we all *know* there was a disturbance. Do 'the signs' tell you anything we don't know already?" Horace sighed as he removed his glasses and rubbed his eyes.

Mab was in a frenzy, flying around in rapid circles, occasionally bouncing off a wall like an addled moth. Willa could barely make out her sharp little voice.

"We've ... got ... to DO something!"

Robert sat sullenly in the corner, punctuating the hubbub with the occasional crashing stomp of a hoof. Fadiyah flapped at the bars of her cage; feathers floated in the air. Even Baz, usually unflappable, was chewing nervously on her bottom lip and moaning.

"The most horrible dreams ... I know something's happening. Something terrible, something absolutely horrid."

Belle countered her, waving her hands in frustration. "Psh. Dreams! Nobody *saw* anything!"

Willa nervously cleared her throat. "I saw something." No one paid her any attention, so she tried again. "I woke up and looked outside...."

"Stop that infernal stomping!" Belle hissed at Robert.

"Shut your trap, you old sea-cow!" he growled back.

Willa took a deep breath and shouted. "I SAW SOMETHING!"

Everyone froze, looking at her. Willa felt suddenly nervous. Her voice faltered. "I — I saw something. I think it's important."

Horace leaned past Willa and shouted up the staircase. "Miss Trang! Come at once!" He led Willa to an armchair. Miss Trang appeared in the doorway in a flash, looking strangely worn and tired. Willa could hardly believe she'd ever been afraid of the woman.

Miss Trang knelt before her and looked her in the eyes. "What did you see, Willa?"

"A black horse with red eyes, running down my street. Running up on two legs!"

Miss Trang blinked in surprise. The others murmured anxiously. She stood suddenly and turned to leave the room, barking, "Come with me, Willa."

Willa followed, wondering if she'd done something wrong. Miss Trang led her into her office and shut the door. She sat at her desk and began writing, speaking to Willa without turning to look at her.

"I have to go away for a few days. I'm leaving right away. You will be in charge. You'll find money for groceries in here." She gestured briefly to a desk drawer. "It would be best if you slept here as well."

Willa stared in astonishment. "In charge? Me? But I ... I don't ..."

Miss Trang spun around in her chair and looked her in the eyes again. She didn't look tired anymore; she looked steely and determined. "You are in charge. Keep the others in line. Don't let the place fall apart. I don't have time to give you the full story, but this is very, very important. All right? Will you help us?"

Willa swallowed. She didn't know what was going on. She felt uneasy and fearful, but this was the first time she'd ever been needed for something important.

She nodded. "Yes, I will."

Chapter Seven

Willa in charge

Miss Trang's departure lifted the dark clouds of worry from the household. As she strode purposefully away up the street with only a small black bag in hand, the old folks relaxed into smiles. The house itself seemed to heave a sigh of relief. Willa watched Miss Trang until she was just a black dot in the distance. She felt Horace's hand on her shoulder.

"No need to worry now. Miss Trang will know what to do." His voice was warm and reassuring.

"But where is she going?"

Horace gestured vaguely. "She's meeting with the others. They'll ... they'll take care of things."

"What others? Who?"

"Oh, beings who are much more important and powerful than this sad group you see here."

He turned to look at the others settling in for tea, chattering away and rattling cups without a care in the world. Mab sat on the mantle swinging her feet and whistling cheerfully. Robert was telling knock-knock jokes and Belle was rolling her eyes good-naturedly. Baz appeared with a plate of scones fresh from the oven and Horace hurried over to get his share.

Willa sank into a chair and watched them. She was glad that whatever was going on was being taken care of, supposedly, somewhere and by someone, but she still had her own worries. First there was the "being in charge" assignment which sat cold and anxious in the pit of her stomach. Looking after this crew seemed far beyond her capabilities. Miss Trang had advised her not to let Robert get his hands on any alcohol, and to take especially good care of Mab. Other than that, "you're in charge" was all she had to say on the matter. But how could Willa be in charge if she had no idea what was going on? Almost as worrying was Miss Trang's insistence that Willa move in until she got back. What was her mom going to say about that?

"Oh, I don't think so, honey. I mean, you're only twelve."

In the past, Willa would have taken this as the final word and gone off to sulk in her room. But now, buoyed by the urgency of the situation and Miss Trang's surprising confidence in her, she actually argued back.

"It means more pay. It's just so Miss Trang won't worry about them. They're old, they need help, and what if there's an emergency in the middle of the night? It's only for a few days, and it's not far away. I'll call you right away if I need help." Her mom said nothing, thinking. Willa pressed on. "Miss Trang is really depending on me. Please can I stay there? Please?"

Then, to her great surprise, her mom relented ... with one condition. She wanted to visit the house and meet everyone. Case the joint with a mother's suspicious eye. Just what Willa was afraid of.

Nobody else shared her fear.

"That shouldn't be a problem. We can have both your parents over for dinner," suggested Horace.

"Will there actually be food?" Willa turned to Baz, who rolled her eyes.

"Ha-ha. Very funny. Of course there will be food. I'll make my roast duck with mashed garlic potatoes and all the trimmings."

Horace nodded. "It's very good."

The next afternoon Willa picked up the items on Baz's grocery list and rushed about "parent-proofing" the house. She hid away the weird, supernatural knick-knacks. She was extra sweet to Mab before shutting her away in her dollhouse. She begged Tengu not to challenge her dad to any manner of combat, suggesting that remarks about the weather might be a better icebreaker. She elicited solemn promises from Belle and Horace to behave themselves and not throw things at each other. She enticed Robert to stay in his room for the evening with a bucket of fried chicken. And she made Baz promise again that she would serve actual, real food. When the doorbell finally rang that evening, delicious smells were issuing from the kitchen. Belle, Horace, and Tengu sat prim and proper in the parlour, and Willa was beginning to think this evening might go very well indeed.

On the way to the door her eye caught Fadiyah in her cage in the corner. Her presence might cause difficulties. Willa's dad was an avid bird watcher. One look at this glittering, exotic creature and he'd be all keen to identify it, and who knew where that might lead. Willa decided it would be safest to put her out of sight. She asked Horace to take Fadi upstairs and went to let her parents in.

They were bearing gifts. Dad had a bottle of Scotch and Mom had brought some homemade cookies and a catnip toy.

"You told me there was a cat," she explained when Willa looked blankly at the toy.

"Oh ... yeah ... right." Willa mumbled her way through the introductions.

Tengu bowed and shook her dad's hand vigorously. "A pleasure, really a pleasure, I have to say. How's the latest weather system been treating you, sir?"

Belle sat sullenly in the corner. She grunted in greeting and stared rather rudely at Willa's mom, who looked distinctly uncomfortable. Luckily, Horace rejoined them just in time to carry the small talk, and Willa hurried into the kitchen to check on Baz.

Everything seemed to be under control. The duck was almost done and everything smelled absolutely amazing.

"You can leave that here." Baz nodded toward the cat toy in Willa's hand.

In the parlour Tengu was wolfing down cookies. *Well, at least that will keep him from saying anything too weird,* thought Willa. Horace and Dad were chatting about gardening like they were old friends. Mom and Belle eyed each other silently from across the room. Willa was just trying to think of something to say when there was a loud stomping from upstairs. Her heart sank. Robert!

Horace leaned over to whisper in her ear. "Perhaps I shouldn't have put the bird in his room."

"Is there someone else here?" asked Mom, looking up at the ceiling.

Willa fidgeted nervously in her chair. "Uh, yeah, that's Robert. He's ... sick in bed. The flu. Highly contagious. Didn't want to infect everybody."

Her dad smiled sympathetically. "Poor guy, that's tough." There was another hoof stomp from upstairs. The chandelier rattled.

"Maybe you should look in on him, dear," suggested her mother, but at that moment there was another crash, from the kitchen this time.

Willa jumped to her feet. "I'd better check on Baz first," she said as calmly as she could, then turned and fled into the kitchen.

The oven door was open. The roasting pan was upended on the floor. A greasy trail led to Baz, also on the floor, smiling blissfully with the duck in her lap. She was picking from the carcass and shoving the bits into her full mouth. Her eyes were mere slits and her head lolled drunkenly. Her free hand clutched the catnip toy.

Willa leaned against the counter, taking in the scene. It was all very simple, actually, once she put the pieces together. She frowned at Baz.

"So *you're* the cat!"

Baz stopped licking her fingers and grinned for a moment before answering in her most velvety voice. "Meow."

After a full minute of panic Willa pulled herself together and devised a plan of attack. First she phoned for pizza delivery. Then she wrested the catnip away from Baz, who put up quite a struggle. She threw what was left of the duck into a plastic bag, which she tucked under her arm as she hauled Baz to her feet and ushered her out through the parlour to the stairs.

"Baz isn't feeling well. Probably caught Robert's flu. Just getting her to her room."

Willa surprised herself at the ease with which she fibbed. Nobody paid much attention to her, though. Tengu giggled in the corner while Mom stared silently at Belle with a strange look of suspicion and anger. Belle looked back warily, defensive now. What had happened? Horace leaned back in his chair, Tengu reached for another cookie, and … Dad was missing!

Willa fairly flew into the hall, where Dad was coming down the stairs.

"Just thought I'd take your sick friend that bottle. There's nothing a shot of premium single malt won't cure."

"You … *gave* it to him?" Willa's head reeled. Her dad could be a little clueless, but surely even he should have noticed that Robert was half horse.

"I just knocked and left it outside his door."

Willa sighed with relief as her dad returned to the parlour. By the time she had hustled Baz up the stairs and into her room (giving her the duck to keep her happy) the bottle had disappeared from outside Robert's door. She knocked and peeked inside. Robert was sitting back on his hind legs in the corner opposite the birdcage. He leaned an elbow on the table strewn with chicken bones and glared across the room at the bird, gripping the bottle in much the same way that Baz had been clutching the catnip.

"Damn thing keeps staring at me!" snarled Robert, taking a swig from the bottle as he flung a bone at the cage. It bounced off the bars and Fadiyah's eyes narrowed.

Willa hurried over and struggled to lift the cage, which was dreadfully heavy. "You know you shouldn't be drinking. Miss Trang said so."

Robert hugged the Scotch tighter to his chest and pouted. Willa rolled her eyes impatiently. "Look, I'll make a deal with you. You can keep the bottle and I won't even tell Miss Trang, if you'll just stay in here and be quiet. Okay? Deal?"

Robert nodded and Willa dragged the cage out of the room. She thought about putting it in Baz's room, but a cat and a bird in one room was probably just asking for trouble. She shoved the cage into the library and hurried back downstairs.

Now her mom and Belle were ignoring each other completely, staring icily into space. Willa's heart sank. Horace and Dad glanced at them uncomfortably. Tengu was laughing so hard, he fell right off the ottoman he was perched on.

"What happened? Did they fight?" Willa whispered. Both her dad and Horace shook their heads in utter bewilderment.

"No. They haven't said a single word."

Willa looked back at Belle and her mom in surprise and for a split second was struck by their identical expressions; stony and unforgiving. *That's the end of my staying here*, she thought. And the thought of letting Miss Trang down pained her more than she ever would have expected.

The pizza arrived and Willa tried to make the best of the meal. She still served the carrots and beans, and the garlic mashed potatoes, carefully smoothing over where her elbow had gone in while she was pulling Baz to her feet. It seemed like a rather bizarre menu. Horace and Belle both raised their eyebrows but said nothing. Surprisingly, her mom and dad seemed genuinely impressed when she gave them her apologies.

"That was quick thinking, Willa, ordering pizza. Well done," her dad offered.

The rest of the evening went a lot smoother, since Willa had rolled Belle to be seated as far as possible from her mom. Dad, as diplomatic as ever, endeavoured to smooth things over with the old lady, and Belle reacted by turning on the charm as well. Horace in turn was impressing her mom with his encyclopedic knowledge of ancient history. Tengu crouched on his chair, his attention focussed solely on picking the mushrooms off his pizza slices and dropping them on the floor. Willa was finally able to sit back and relax a little. As she was leaving with her parents for home, however, Belle and her mom gave each other another long, icy look before Horace could wheel the old dame away.

They walked in silence and darkness, moving in and out of the pools of streetlight. Willa's mom seemed totally lost in thought. Finally, in front of their house Willa could stand it no longer.

"So … is it okay? Can I stay there nights?"

Her dad tipped his head doubtfully and looked at her mom, who snapped out of her reverie at the question.

"Oh, right. I, uh …" Willa was surprised. Her mom hadn't even been thinking about the issue. What was on her mind?

Dad jumped to her defence. "I thought you showed a lot of maturity there, Willa. Saving dinner and all. And looking after those poor old dears when they get sick. I was very impressed." He put his arm around her shoulder and gave her a little squeeze. Willa smiled. Good old Dad. They both turned to Mom, expectant.

She gazed at the two of them for a moment and suddenly looked very tired. "Yes, you managed wonderfully. I think this is a good experience for you." She paused. "You can stay there starting tomorrow, but if anything gets out of hand you give us a call, any time of the day or night, all right?"

Willa couldn't believe her ears. She nodded eagerly. "Okay, I will. Thanks, Mom! Thanks, Dad!"

"Only ..." her mom wasn't finished, "... about Belle. She's ... I wouldn't trust her, honey. Just try to avoid her if you can. I mean it. Watch out for her." And with that she turned on her heel and strode up to the front door.

Willa and Dad exchanged puzzled looks as Mom jangled the keys in the lock.

"They didn't say *anything* to each other?" whispered Willa.

Her dad shook his head. "Not a word."

Willa's mom disappeared into the dark house.

Chapter Eight

Willa moves in and the place falls apart

The next morning Willa woke with a foggy brain. Her limbs felt heavy and slow. She had slept very strangely, a deep, smothering kind of sleep, with no dreams.

She packed a small bag of essentials and headed over to the boarding house, yawning all the way. She couldn't shake off the drowsiness.

The house was very quiet, which made Willa uneasy. Belle sat in the upstairs hall, gloomily staring out at the backyard. Willa asked her which room she should stay in.

Belle shrugged. "I don't care. Suit yourself."

Willa chose a turret room on the top floor. It was smaller than the other rooms, but she liked it because it was round and had a little window seat with a worn red velvet cushion. She peered out the window, down at the people in the street. Ordinary people going to the store or work. Ordinary kids biking to the park and meeting up with their friends. They seemed very far away, like she was watching them through a telescope. She unpacked her clothes and toothbrush and such, and went in search of the others.

Horace was in the library as usual, but his book lay open and unread in his lap as he snoozed with his head propped in his hand. Fadiyah was hopping about restlessly on her perch. Willa put her hand on the bars of the cage and the bird stopped and looked at her. As usual, waves of reassurance wafted over her, like a gentle breeze. She took a deep breath and felt calm. The bird nodded.

Baz was still asleep. Willa could hear her snoring through the heavy door. Robert's room, however, was empty. Willa hurried back to Belle, still at the window.

"Belle! Where's Robert?"

The old lady raised an eyebrow. "Oh, Robert had a fine time last night, thanks to the Scotch. You should have heard him carrying on … the old goat."

"But where is he? Where did he go?"

Belle nodded toward the yard. "He was partying with the floozies back there."

"Who?" Willa was confused.

"The wood nymphs," Belle answered wearily as she wheeled away. "I need a nap."

Tengu was in the dining room with his head down on the table, fast asleep. Willa gently shook his arm.

"Tengu! Wake up! We have to go find Robert."

He lifted his bleary head and blinked. "Okay."

"Why is everyone so tired? How late did you stay up?"

"Oh, I went to bed right away, but I didn't sleep well. Don't feel rested at all."

"I had the same kind of night." Willa yawned, and they went out the kitchen door into the misty back garden.

The stable was straight ahead, in the back left corner of the property, but it could barely be seen, covered in ivy and drowning in tall grass. To the right of the stable was a stand of trees, strung heavily with vines and moss. Further to the right, next to the high fence that separated them from the Hacketts, was an open sunny area, but it was so clogged with grasses and prickly blackberry bushes that it was even more impassable than the woods.

Tengu led the way into the trees, following the loud sound of snoring. He pushed aside the branches and thorns for Willa, but she still found it hard to keep up with the agile little man. Once she heard a strange breath, like a sigh, that came from all sides at once. It sounded ancient and sad and chilled her to the bone. She hurried to catch up to Tengu, who was waiting for her.

"You'd better stick with me. Don't want you wandering off on your own. You might fall in the pool or something."

"There's a pool?"

He waved vaguely toward the open area. "Yes, but it's all grown over, full of weeds and slimy things. Best left alone." They continued on.

Finally, beside the stable, they came upon a very strange sight. Robert was sound asleep sitting against the stone wall. Lying on the ground around him were a couple dozen little fairies, also asleep. With their long hair matted and their leafy clothing in severe disarray, they looked like discarded dolls. All was quiet except for snoring, Robert's booming and the wood nymphs' squeaky little snorts.

Willa couldn't help but laugh. "So these are wood nymphs!"

Tengu nodded, also giggling a little. "A real disgrace, they are."

Willa always had an eye on the Hackett house. To her relief the corner of the garden where Robert and the nymphs were passed out was shielded from the neighbours' sight by thick vines and branches. However, they had to traverse a rather open area of the yard to get back in the house, so she fetched a blanket to throw over Robert's head and shoulders. It was quite a struggle, but they finally got him to his feet, or his hooves, and he lurched toward the back door, moaning and grumbling.

Willa could see Mr. and Mrs. Hackett sitting in their kitchen, and when Robert's hooves hit the back steps with a loud thud, Mr. Hackett leaned to peer out the window at them. Pulling the blanket firmly over Robert's head, Willa and Tengu desperately shoved him into the kitchen, resulting in more crashing and cursing. Willa was stumbling up the steps, about to follow them inside, when she heard Mr. Hackett.

"Oh, Willaaaa!" He was on the back step now, hands on his hips. He wore that smug look that could only mean he had a grievance.

Willa sighed and conjured up a cheerful expression. "Hello, Mr. Hackett."

"Was that a horse I just saw? It's against zoning to have livestock, you know."

"No, no," Willa laughed nervously. "It's not a real horse, just a costume. We, uh, had a costume party last night. I hope we didn't make too much noise." She knew the mention of noise would divert Mr. Hackett's attention away from Robert. Noise was one of his favourite topics. She was right.

"Indeed! An unholy row it was, and after midnight too!" He was just getting revved up when Mrs. Hackett popped her head out the door.

"Later than that. I looked at my bedside clock and it said one thirty-seven precisely. I remember. One thirty-seven."

"It's really unacceptable, Willa," continued Mr. Hackett. "I very nearly called the police."

"Oh, thank you for not calling. It won't happen again. We won't have any more parties, I promise."

"I should hope not," sniffed Mrs. Hackett, patting her curlers and disappearing inside. Mr. Hackett remained, still peering curiously at the house. Willa smiled brightly, edging away.

"Welllll, anyway ... sorry for your trouble. Have a nice day!" As she opened the kitchen door there was another loud crash from inside. She gave Mr. Hackett another smile and a shrug, and hurried inside.

Robert had paused for a breather, leaning against the kitchen wall, and Tengu was picking up the chairs he'd knocked over. Willa took a deep breath, collecting her thoughts.

"Okay. We'll get Robert up to his room where he can sleep it off." Robert merely grunted in reply and rubbed his eyes. Willa squinted out the window. "I hope the nymphs are all right out there."

"They'll have to be," replied Tengu. "We can't bring them in here. They don't get along with Mab *at all*. Some kind of fairy feud."

Willa froze. "Omigosh. Mab!"

Rushing into the parlour, she retrieved the tiny key from the mantlepiece and paused before the dollhouse. She'd locked Mab in there before dinner last night and had forgotten to let her out again. She unclicked the lock and swung the side of the house open to see Mab sitting on the bed, arms crossed and staring daggers at her. The fairy's face was purple with rage. Willa stuttered her apologies but Mab silently glared her down. Willa was relieved for the distraction of Robert clip-clopping through the house, moaning piteously. She joined Tengu, watching helplessly as the centaur staggered up the stairs, leaning against the wall or the bannister, which creaked under his weight, threatening imminent collapse. At the top he knocked a painting off the wall, slumped around the corner, and finally disappeared into his room.

Willa sighed. "No more booze for Robert."

Willa awoke the next morning to the strangest sound she'd ever heard, like a trumpet being strangled. She opened her eyes and had a moment of confusion, taking in the dark, musty room instead of her bright, clean room at home. Then she remembered where she was, and knew the noise to be Tengu greeting the day with his rooster impression. She looked up at the ceiling, and her brain felt just as dusty, cracked, and cobwebby as the room around her. This was the second night she hadn't had any dreams, and her head felt like it was filled with mud. Every thought required great effort and she felt vaguely anxious.

She moved clumsily down the stairs. It was like she was on a planet with a force of gravity that made her weigh twice as much as she did on Earth, only she couldn't remember whether it was small planets or big planets that would do that. Her thoughts were scattered and leaden. It was only when she glanced over at Fadiyah, serene and dignified in her cage in the parlour, that she felt calm and capable again.

In the dining room it was evident that she wasn't the only one who was having trouble waking up. Belle was snoring in her chair in the corner, her head tipped back and mouth open. Horace stared blankly into space and rubbed his temples.

"Good morning," Willa ventured, just as the kitchen door swung open and banged her elbow. Baz shuffled in with the teapot and cups on a tray. She paused to yawn, her hands shaking with the force of it, and tea slopped onto the floor.

Nobody had much to say, other than that they were all sleeping poorly and without dreams, just like Willa. And it was taking its toll. Even the normally chipper Tengu was subdued. Robert didn't get out of bed until noon, but that could have been due to the crashing hangover he claimed to still have. Mab, on the other hand, seemed energetic enough, even spritely. Willa was positive she caught a smirk on her face when the others complained about being tired. Mab was still mad, though, about being locked up, and wouldn't speak to anyone.

Over the next few days Willa wearily struggled to keep up with her duties, only leaving the house to buy groceries and to go home one night for dinner. At the table she could barely keep up a conversation and yawned so much her parents were alarmed.

"How hard are those oldsters working you?" her dad wanted to know. "Aren't you getting enough sleep?"

Willa insisted that she was. In fact, she was going to bed embarrassingly early these days, at eight or nine o'clock.

And she wasn't the only one. Everyone in the house was sleeping in later each day, napping frequently through the day, and heading upstairs to go to bed at earlier and earlier hours in the evening, yet with each passing day they grew more tired. Conversations became rare and made little to no sense as everyone forgot what they were about to say. They were all clumsier, stumbling and dropping things. Even the bird stared with dull eyes and wobbled on her perch, nearly falling off.

On the fifth day of this sleepiness Willa felt a need for some fresh air to clear her head and ventured out into the backyard jungle. She had waited until she saw the Hacketts leave in their car. She wanted to be alone and not have to chit-chat with those two. Keeping in mind the overgrown pool Tengu said was back there, she proceeded very cautiously, probing the tangled weeds ahead of her with a long stick. The air was thick and muggy, and her hair started to stick to her forehead and the back of her neck.

She soon reached the clearing. It was low-lying and rather soggy underfoot, so she was glad to spot a large, sloping grey stone emerging from the damp moss. She clambered up on it and sat down to think. She was worried. Why were they all so tired? It didn't seem normal. Was a magic spell causing it? Was this being done by the enemies Horace had spoken about? Willa wished Miss Trang would get back soon. She'd know what to do.

Willa yawned. She lay back on the rock and yawned again, the kind of yawn that makes you wonder if it's ever going to end. And when it finally did end she heard someone yawn back. Or rather she *felt* it. The yawn surrounded her and vibrated through her body, a yawn so big and deep that she sat up in alarm. The rock beneath her was shifting.

An earthquake! she thought, and scrambled off, but the ground was still. She poked the rock with her stick and it shuddered.

Her heart beat wildly. The yard was silent, still. She wanted to run into the house and call the others, but ... she couldn't help herself. She inched forward through the thick brush, uncovering more of the rock — or whatever it was — and repeatedly poking it with the stick. Each time she did it twitched and rippled a little, like a muscle flexing. When she found the edge of the thing, she proceeded around its perimeter, which turned out to be a perfect, straight-edged rectangle. It was the pool. But a pool should be a hole in the ground, and this was a mound, a perfectly rectangular mound. It took Willa's weary brain a moment or two to come up with the answer. The pool was filled with something large, grey, and leathery. Something that yawned and moved. It was time to get the others.

They gathered around the thing, wrinkling their noses against the stench of the brackish water. Flies buzzed around them and the air was strangely still. To her surprise, nobody else knew anything about it, or had any guess as to what it could be. They gathered around while Tengu and Horace cut back the foliage. Even so, it was hard to make out any details. The thing had creases that contained slimy green water, and folds craggy with moss, but most of its bulk was smooth and grey. Horace pointed out what looked to be a long neck folded alongside the body, and to where the head probably was, tucked out of sight. They tentatively ran their hands over the "skin." It was smoother than stone, almost leathery. Was it a kind of huge snake? A lizard? A smooth-skinned crocodile? Whatever it was, it had taken refuge in the water of the pool, and it had been there a long, long time.

"So it came here before any of you did. How long have you all been here?" asked Willa. They pondered this question, brows furrowed.

Horace waved vaguely. "It's rather hard to say. I'm never sure about how fast time is passing here...."

Willa was confused. "Well who's been here the longest?"

Belle shook her head. "Not me. I arrived last. I'm ..." and here she started to cackle, "... the baby of the group."

Horace spoke again, looking pained. "I can't remember for sure, but I might have been the first, although I remember Miss Trang from those days."

Willa was getting impatient. "What days? How long ago?"

Horace shrugged. "It could be decades. Or centuries. Or millennia. I'm sorry, but they all feel the same to me." He gestured to the house. "Places like this ... Where we come from time moves differently. When we retired the only way we could live in your ... time ... was to come to a safehouse with a special time-regulating dispensation...."

Willa gave up trying to understand. Horace was being strangely unhelpful, going on and not making sense when they had this ... this *thing* in front of them. This monstrous *thing*.

"So what is it? Is it dangerous? Should we get it out of there?" Willa asked. No one had an answer.

A sudden loud screech echoed around the yard, making them jump. It was Fadiyah, up above them in her cage. Willa had put the bird out on a third floor balcony so she could get some air. She'd never heard Fadi make a sound like this before. Everyone stared up as Fadi screamed, each squawk increasing in pitch, volume, and intensity until they had to turn away and hold their ears. Willa thanked her lucky stars that the Hacketts weren't home. They would not like this racket one bit.

It felt like the sound was drilling right into Willa's brain. She pressed her palms hard into her ears and dropped to her knees. When she thought she couldn't take another moment, the earth rumbled and the bird went quiet. The shape in the pool writhed. Willa stumbled back, grabbing at Belle's wheelchair and yanking her back too.

The grey beast shifted from side to side, the concrete of the pool popping and cracking, then it slowly lifted its long neck, raising its head from the muck. It had a lizard-like face, a wide mouth and huge, moist eyes with long lashes. Its grey skin lay in folds like an elephant's, but it certainly wasn't an elephant. Willa felt a wild, insane excitement, and actually laughed out loud. Just when she thought this place couldn't get any weirder, there turned out to be a dinosaur in the swimming pool.

Chapter Nine

Wearier and wearier, Willa solves a mystery

As they stared at it in shock, the dinosaur swung its drooping head back and forth, taking in the entire scene with sleepy eyes. It didn't seem dangerous. Willa devoutly hoped it was a herbivore. Then the beast spotted the bird up on the balcony and slowly lifted its head, coughing wheezily. When it finally reached the third floor, the dinosaur squinted briefly at the bird. Then its eyes rolled back in its head and it flopped to the ground with a terrific crash.

Willa stared in shock. Had the only dinosaur alive in the whole world just died in front of her? They approached cautiously. Horace gingerly put a hand on its neck and announced it still had a pulse. He guessed it had simply fainted.

Willa's next big problem was how to keep a full-sized dinosaur out of sight of the neighbours. The bushes provided only partial cover, so Willa dashed to the hardware store for enormous blue tarps and several long poles. Tengu helped her fashion a large tent over the pool, and they worked quickly in the heat and humidity while Horace sat and watched.

The dinosaur came to as they worked and watched them calmly. Its long lashes convinced Willa it was a she, and she began calling her Dinah. Willa was concerned about Dinah's health, since she didn't seem to be able to climb out of the pool. Horace speculated she'd been immobile in the pool for a good long while and this had probably caused her legs to weaken. Willa asked how she could have got there, and where was she before, and how old was she anyway? At this Horace got all vague again, talking about different kinds of time and something called a time talisman, and "rips in the fabric of time," until Willa simply gave up asking questions.

However Dinah had gotten in the pool, she'd been there a while, and Horace maintained that her legs may have become "vestigial," or permanently useless. Willa hoped not. She hoped beyond hope that she could see Dinah walking around like she would have done millions of years ago. But they'd have to work up to that and allow her to regain her strength. She did not look at all well at the moment, sniffling and wheezing, but hopefully time and rest would put her right.

Luckily they got the tent up before the Hacketts returned home late that afternoon. It blocked the entire pool area from their view, though it wasn't tall enough to cover Dinah if she was ever able to stand up. Predictably, Mr. Hackett appeared on his back step, squinting over at the tent and shaking his head in irritation. And Mrs. Hackett squawked out the kitchen window that the thing was a "terrible eyesore," but Willa knew there was nothing much they could do about it.

That evening Willa sat at the dining room table, surrounded by library books about dinosaurs. Curiosity drew the others to the table.

Robert peered over Willa's shoulder. "What is she, exactly?"

"I think she's a Diplodocus," Willa announced. Dinah wasn't exactly like the pictures in the book, not as big for one thing, but it was the closest match she could find. "She's a plant eater."

"Well, that's a relief," muttered Belle, squinting at the page. "She's got the same tiny head as the picture. Not much room for a brain in there."

"All the dinosaurs had small brains. Dinah's neck is so long that if her head was any bigger, she wouldn't be able to lift it at all," answered Willa. "As it is she can really only hold her neck horizontally. She can't lift it up vertically."

"Why not?" asked Tengu.

"Her heart isn't big enough to pump blood all the way up to her head if she did. That's probably why she fainted when she did try to lift her head up." She turned back to the book and read on. "Some scientists think that to lift their heads up high dinosaurs like these would have to have a second heart in their neck to do the job...."

"That is the silliest thing I ever heard. No wonder the poor bastards died out," grumbled Robert.

"Not all of them did," grinned Willa.

The dinosaur lifted everyone's mood for a few days. Forgetting their exhaustion and cloudy sleep, the old folks chatted endlessly about the beast. They speculated on her history and how she had survived for so long. Horace said she must have stayed alive by drinking the green muck growing in the rainwater which collected in the low area around the pool. But since her food intake was so reduced, she had slipped into a kind of hibernation. A long, *long* hibernation.

As the next few days slipped by, Dinah showed no signs of wanting to climb out of the pool, preferring to sleep away her days. The novelty of their new pet abated and everyone fell back into a tired funk. Willa was left with the chore of piling up as much greenery — garden clippings, leaves, kitchen food waste — as she could find for Dinah. The dinosaur's appetite was on the rise since waking. Willa had to spend a couple of hours every day pruning the huge garden and tossing the clippings into a heap. Then she'd give Dinah's back a scratch with the garden rake. Dinah would slowly lift her head, snuffling and blinking her long-lashed cow-eyes. She'd nod a few times as she looked around, slowly zeroing in on Willa and the pile of branches, then she'd move in and gulp it all down in a few seconds.

The rest of the time she grazed on whatever she could reach, stripping leaves and bark from branches with alarming efficiency. Willa worried about her devouring all the greenery which kept her shielded from prying Hackett eyes. She also worried about Dinah's long neck. She hoped the books were right about her not being able to lift her head, because that meant she wouldn't be able to peek over the fence ... Willa didn't even want to think about the hysteria that would certainly follow *that!* As it was she could see that keeping Dinah much longer in their backyard was impossible.

"What'll we do with her?" she asked the others, but they were slipping back into sleepy apathy. A shrug from Baz, silence from Horace, a derisive snort from Robert. Only Belle came up with a remotely useful idea.

"She's from the water, isn't she? Throw her in the ocean. Let her fend for herself."

"Fine," countered Willa. "But how do we get a sixty-foot dinosaur from our backyard to the seashore without anyone seeing?"

Nobody had an answer for that one. Nobody had much of an answer for anything anymore. Exhaustion levels were rising higher and higher. Horace fell asleep face down in his books. Belle stared into space, her eyes glazed over. Baz didn't cook at all anymore but slept for most of the day, curled up on the carpet in the parlour. Willa had to do everything herself now, making sandwiches and tea for them all, piling up brush for the dinosaur, and cleaning up after everyone. They were constantly spilling things, dropping things, and breaking things by dozing off at inopportune moments. Willa did her best to keep up with the work, when all she wanted to do was go to sleep herself.

One afternoon, a few days after the discovery of Dinah, Willa took a break from her chores to collapse into an armchair in the parlour. She rubbed her eyes and stared dully at the doll's house. She could hear Mab humming cheerfully in there, clicking away with her knitting needles. Mab alone seemed immune to the weariness of the household. She kept to herself but buzzed around with her usual energy. Willa's head hurt as she puzzled over this. Why wasn't Mab tired? The rest of them hadn't slept properly since ... since the dinner party with her parents. When she'd accidentally left Mab locked in the dollhouse. Mab was still not talking to her, still mad about that.

Willa sat up. Her brain cleared a bit and things started falling into place. She rose and opened the dollhouse. Mab scowled at her from the sofa, where she was knitting her silvery scarf.

"Mab, I need to ask you something." Mab squinted her eyes into slits, but Willa went on. "None of us are getting any rest when we sleep. I'm not sure why. We sleep and sleep but we're still tired."

Mab rolled her eyes in irritation. "It's not the sleep, it's the dreams!" she snapped.

Willa thought this over. "We're sleeping but we're not dreaming. And that's why we're so tired?"

Mab gave her a look. Willa pressed on. "You are the only one in this house who isn't tired. You're the only one who's still dreaming, aren't you?"

Mab let out a noncommittal squeak and turned away, clickety-clacking with her knitting needles.

Willa spoke sharply. "Mab!"

The fairy turned back, looking like a child who's been caught with her hand in the cookie jar. Willa softened her tone.

"Mab, please. Do you know why we're not dreaming?" Mab dropped her eyes and nodded. "Are you the one who's causing it?" Another nod. "What are you doing? Can you undo it?" A shrug and Mab turned away again. Willa waited a moment, then quietly closed the dollhouse again. She felt a wave of relief. At least their weariness wasn't the result of sinister forces. Just a peeved fairy.

Later that evening Willa gathered everyone in the parlour. She knelt by the dollhouse. "Oh Maa-aab," she called softly. "May we come in?"

The clicking needles stopped. Willa waited a moment and opened the dollhouse. Mab looked surprised to see everyone.

"Mab, I'm so sorry I left you locked up after the dinner party. I promise I won't ever do it again." Willa held out the dollhouse's tiny key and set it gently on the bed.

Horace cleared his throat gently. "We're all sorry, Mab. We're sorry we don't treat you with the respect you deserve." Mab looked expectantly at the others, who begrudgingly nodded ... even Belle. Baz produced a small tray filled with tiny cakes and real, Mab-sized teacups and saucers.

"Sorry, dearie," Baz smiled as she set the tray carefully inside the dollhouse.

Mab picked up a teacup, turning it over in her hands. Willa had noticed that Mab drank from thimbles, so she had scoured the stores for a teeny tea service. Mab appreciated it, she could tell, for the little fairy hugged the cup to her chest, sniffling a little and not looking up.

"Can you forgive us? Can you forgive *me?*" Willa pleaded.

Mab wiped her nose with the back of her hand and looked up at them all, her eyes glistening. She nodded quickly.

That night Willa slept. She really slept, and dreamed. The dreams fell from her mind as she opened her eyes to the early morning light, but she felt light and happy. The heavy curtain of exhaustion had lifted. She practically bounced out of bed.

In the dining room Willa saw a rare and welcome sight. Robert and Belle were chatting amiably over toast and jam. Tengu stopped shovelling down scrambled eggs to wave cheerfully, and Horace nodded and grinned. Baz bustled in from the kitchen, dumping fresh-baked scones into a basket. Tengu grabbed three and began juggling them. The mood was one of barely-contained giddiness. Willa took a seat.

"I trust you slept well?" inquired Horace.

Willa nodded. "And I dreamed, too."

"So did I." Horace nodded thoughtfully. "I dreamt I was looking out the window at something ... a horse, I think."

Something shifted in Willa's memory and she felt suddenly chilled. Her own dream was reassembling itself in her mind. A black night, a white moon, a pounding sound, a dark shape in the streetlight.

"A black horse," she whispered. Silence fell over the table. She looked around. The smiles had faded.

"A black horse!"

"Yes! Me too!"

"Now I remember!"

"With red eyes!"

Baz sank into a chair, looking worried. "How could we all have the same dream?"

Willa looked around at them all. "That black horse is the same one I saw before Miss Trang left. A black horse with red eyes that ran down the street on two legs." Her hands were cold and trembled in her lap at the memory.

"Indeed," murmured Horace. "And now he's shown up in our dreams. He's been looking for us."

Belle finished his thought, speaking in a low, hoarse voice. "And now he's found us."

Horace nodded. Willa's heart sank.

Chapter Ten

Augury and Fog

"But he's just in our dreams ... is he real? Why was he looking for us? What's he going to do? What should *we* do?"

Willa looked anxiously to Horace, who was frowning and staring into his tea. The whole group waited in silence for a long moment while he thought. Finally, he cleared his throat.

"The horse is a Grant, and yes, he is real. All too real. However, we don't need to worry about *him* so much. He was sent to find us and his job is done."

"He was *sent*?" Willa fought to keep calm.

"The Grant is sent by his masters to scout about and find people. When you saw him that first time, Miss Trang knew it was a bad sign, that something evil was brewing, but she never thought he might be searching for *us*. If she had, she wouldn't have left."

Horace took a sip of his tea before going on. "But now ... now it appears that he *was* looking for us. He roamed the streets and roads of the dreamworld, searching. When Mab stopped us from dreaming, without knowing it she also prevented the Grant from being able to find us."

Belle passed a pale hand over her eyes. "And when we were able to dream again, he found us. In our dreams."

Willa leaned forward. "But why was he looking for us? Who sent him?"

Horace straightened his spoon. "The Other Side sent him."

Robert stomped a hoof in irritation, rattling the cups. "Rubbish. What on earth would the Other Side want with a pathetic collection of old farts like us? What good are we to anyone?"

"I ... I'm not sure." Horace rubbed his forehead. He suddenly looked very old. "I need to think...." He struggled to his feet and left the room. The others exchanged worried looks. Willa was still frantic for some answers.

"I don't understand. What's the Other Side?"

Baz started clearing the table. Robert looked out the window. Tengu muttered about things he had to do and slipped out of the room.

Willa appealed to Belle. "What is the Other Side?"

Belle made a face and waved her hand. "Oh, nothing you have to worry about. It's just ... You know, there's this side, and then ..." She mimed lifting a rock and turning it over. "There's the other side. The side you can't see. The underneath."

"But what are we talking about here? Bad guys? Monsters? What?" Willa was feeling panicky now.

"You read too many books," replied Belle sharply, clearly finished with the conversation. "Don't worry about it. I'm sure it's nothing. Like Robert said, they couldn't possibly want anything with us." She turned and wheeled out of the room.

Willa slumped in her chair, exasperated. Belle was treating her like a little kid. Well, she *was* going to worry about it. After all, Miss Trang left her in charge. She sat up suddenly. Miss Trang. Of course. They needed to call her back, and right away!

Willa hurried up the stairs to the library, where she knew she'd find Horace. She felt a little relieved at the thought of Miss Trang. She and Horace would figure everything out. Everything would be fine if they could just get Miss Trang to come home.

Horace was sitting in his usual chair, staring out the window. Willa paused a moment in the doorway. The sight of him there, thinking so intently, comforted her.

She coughed softly. Horace looked up brightly, smiling. "Hello. Is it teatime already?"

Willa felt cold. "No ... we just had breakfast ... I was wondering about the Grant. You said you needed to think?"

Horace blinked. "The Grant. Yes."

Willa approached. "Can you call Miss Trang back? I think we need her help."

Horace considered this for a moment. "Miss Trang. Yes, that would be a good idea. But first I think an augury is called for. Then hopefully I'll have more information to relay to her."

"Augury, you told me about that. Foretelling the future, right?"

"Yes. I'll read the signs, see what's brewing. I'll do it tonight. I just need to find a high point, where I can see as much of the landscape as possible."

"You can see the whole town from the top of Hanlan's Hill, and the ocean too, if it's clear."

"Exactly the spot. Splendid."

"May I come with you? I can show you the way."

"All right. We'll leave at ten."

Later that afternoon Willa came down the stairs and paused in the front hallway. It was strangely dark. A black shadow pooled in one corner. Willa flicked on the hall light, but the shadow didn't disappear in the light. It remained, as if someone had painted it onto the wainscotting — an inky black triangle reaching about a foot up the wall.

Willa knelt and leaned close to stare into the shadow but could see nothing. She gingerly slid her foot into the shadow. The blackness was total. It was like the end of her shoe had just disappeared. Her toes tingled with a cold electrical tickle. There was a sudden skittery scratching noise and she jumped back.

A few minutes later everyone was gathered around the shadow — everyone except Robert, who was asleep in his room. Horace solemnly ran his hand along the wall above and beside the blackness.

"Yes. Yes. Definitely." He sat back, a worried frown on his face.

"Definitely what? What is it?" Willa ventured, afraid of the answer.

"It's a temporal tear, a little rip in time. It's not uncommon in houses such as ours. Especially with the superintendent away. Miss Trang, I mean. You look away for a moment and there it is. The trick is to not let it spread or you're in big trouble. It's a lot like termites, actually."

"I'll bet you anything it was opened up by somebody," muttered Belle darkly.

Horace considered this. "Well ... yes. Simple carelessness could possibly cause it...."

"*Possibly?* It *was* opened by someone and I know who. That old drunk and his little bimbo friends."

Baz was nodding in agreement. "It *had* to be them!"

Even Horace looked convinced. "It *is* possible, maybe while they were imbibing, a careless word or ..."

"I've always said the Bacchantes were a danger to everyone," interrupted Belle. "They belong on the Other Side, not here with civilized beings ..."

"CIVILIZED BEINGS??!" Robert's voice boomed. He stood at the top of the stairs, his face twisted in anger. "*Civilized?* You call yourself *civilized*, you malicious old sea hag?"

Horace blinked anxiously. "Now Robert, we weren't saying — "

"Oh, you weren't? I heard you, Horace, you agreed with her. Why should *I* be under suspicion ..."

"I didn't actually agree ..."

"You did too, you spineless ninny!" bellowed Robert.

Horace started to lose his cool at this, flickering golden in the hall light, turning uncertainly in and out of his lion-shape. Robert started down the stairs, continuing to shout. Belle screeched back at him. Tengu backed away, his hands over his ears, but Baz grinned at the ruckus.

Willa glanced at the black stain. It was slowly sending an inky finger out along the floor.

"Look! Look! It's growing!" she shouted. Everyone froze, looking down at the black shadow.

"We all need to calm down," counselled Willa. "Fighting isn't going to help." She felt like she was talking to four-year-olds. Horace slipped back into his human form, looking sheepish. Belle turned her head away, scowling. Robert sat on the steps, his head in his hands.

In the ensuing silence she could see that the black stain had halted. She looked around at them as they glared darkly at each other. They seemed like strangers to her. Childish, whining, fighting strangers. Just when she needed them to be grown-ups. She couldn't wait for Miss Trang to come back.

The view from Hanlan's Hill was spectacular. The town lay stretched out before them, twinkling and still. The streetlights made it look like a vast airport, with row upon row of landing strips. Beyond the lights all was black, but past that a ribbon of silver marked the horizon: the ocean, caught in the moonlight. Horace said the spot was perfect, and pulled out a long stick with a hook at the end. He traced a circle in the dirt and sat down in the centre. And watched. And waited.

Willa sat on a nearby log, trying to make herself comfortable. Horace had warned her that the augury had to proceed in total silence, which was easier said than done. She was jumpy, nervous, and full of questions. Sitting quietly on a hilltop was the very last thing she wanted to be doing tonight. She had expected an augury to have more ... well, action, or at least swirling mists and crystal ball visions. Instead it involved Horace sitting cross-legged on the ground, staring out at the view. Once in a while he would peer through a small pair of opera glasses, following the flight of seagulls, or an eagle, or little flocks of songbirds. Willa shook her head. Trust Horace to get sidetracked by a few pigeons when he was supposed to be determining whether or not they were in danger!

Willa's head snapped back as she woke with a little snort. She clapped her hands over her mouth but Horace looked back at her and smiled.

"Had enough? Should we head home?"

"No, no. Sorry. I'm fine, we can stay."

Horace was wearily getting to his feet. Willa jumped up to help him. "Quite all right. I believe I'm finished here."

Willa was surprised. "But what did you see? I didn't see anything, apart from a few birds."

"That's what augury is. The signs can be very simple, very subtle. Often just the comings and goings of birds. The direction, speed, numbers, species … it all means something."

Horace rubbed his forehead a little, chagrined. "It's been a good five hundred years since I've attempted this, so I've lost some of my skill for precise prognostication … but generally, here's what I see." His voice dropped lower and lower and Willa leaned close to hear.

"Something coming. Darkness and cold swirling in from all directions. A dam about to burst. Walls giving way to great power and force. And darkness. Everywhere, in everything I see darkness. It's coming."

His voice cracked and fell into silence. He looked down at the ground and his breathing was laboured. Willa said nothing, but took his arm and they turned toward home.

They descended the hill in thoughtful silence, branches crackling underfoot, Horace in front and Willa reaching out to take his arm every time he stumbled. At the bottom they stepped back onto pavement and paused in a pool of streetlight. The city was deathly still, TV light flickering in the windows of the houses around them, and a wispy fog creeping in.

Horace looked around, slowly turning to take in the whole scene.

"Horace? What's wrong?"

He turned, startled, and looked at her in surprise. "Oh! Excuse me miss, but what street is this?"

Willa stared at him. Was he joking? No, he was

114

looking at her with a polite smile on his face. They stood there for a long moment. Willa's heart was in her throat. "Horace. It's me. Willa."

Horace looked steadily at her and blinked a couple of times. Then he took a step back, out of the harsh glare of the streetlight. His face fell into shadow.

"Yes, Willa, sorry, I'm ... I've just gotten turned around. Which way did we come?"

Willa pointed the way and he started off. She followed slowly, stunned. She'd seen that look many times before, when Horace paused and blinked like that. And now she knew what it meant. He was forgetting things and covering it up. Her heart sank. She hurried to catch up to him.

"Horace, can you call Miss Trang? You said you could, can you call her right now?" She was trying not to sound too eager. "You can call her, right?"

Horace didn't look at her as he answered. "Yes ... yes, of course I can. It's just a matter of ... well, it's rather hard to explain. I'll ... I'll do it when we get back. Or maybe in the morning...." His voice trailed away and he quickened his pace.

The fog was growing thicker. They walked through the silent streets, sometimes in light and sometimes in darkness. Willa knew he was covering up again. He didn't want to admit he couldn't remember how to call Miss Trang. Willa felt alone, she felt very alone. She longed for someone else to be in charge. She could help, she could do whatever she was told to do. Anything would be better than everything being so uncertain.

She felt like danger was all around, but she didn't know what kind of danger or what they could possibly do to escape it.

As they turned the final corner Willa's thoughts were interrupted by the sight of the house blanketed in heavy fog and darkness, a cloud of black birds floating overhead.

Chapter Eleven

Dark intruders

Willa quickened her pace, her heart pounding. All the streetlights around the house were out. It was as if a dark veil had been dropped over their corner of the street. Above them hosts of large black birds wheeled silently. The front fence was crowded with them as well. Behind them the bushes were dotted with little sparrows.

As Willa drew closer, she slowed to a stop. She could now see that the sparrows weren't perched there, they were dead and impaled, a spare branch poking out from every still breast.

The bigger birds shifted from foot to foot, watching Willa steadily. The only sound was the rhythmic scrape scraping of their bills rubbing together, like blades being sharpened.

Horace caught up to her and Willa clutched his arm. They edged cautiously past the birds and up the front walk. Lights glowed dimly inside. There was a sudden familiar screech from inside the house.

"Belle! Are you all right?" Willa called out, the door banging shut behind her.

She received no answer, but the ruckus continued from upstairs. It was just another row between Belle and Robert. The light fixtures shook from the impact of his stamping about, and shadows danced everywhere.

Horace leaned to peer at the black pool in the corner. It had grown, a thin tendril of darkness inching up the wall, following the house's corner seam. And that wasn't all. As Willa looked about she began to see tiny black spots here and there on the ceiling, in the corners, at the base of the stairs. She tugged on Horace's sleeve, silently pointing. He blinked and nodded as he took them in, looking lost and old.

Suddenly Robert appeared, crashing down the stairs in a high rage as Belle glared down from the top step. "Harpy! Crone! Shrew!" he roared.

Belle responded with a rather unbecoming raspberry. Horace meekly stood aside as Robert careened toward them, but Willa stood her ground, holding up her hands in entreaty.

"Robert! You can't go now! Please listen to me. Something is coming. Something awful!"

Robert scowled down at her. Belle screeched from the top of the stairs, "Let the old scoundrel go. Good riddance!"

Willa heard scratchy skittering sounds from all around. The black spots along the baseboards were growing larger. She took a deep breath.

"STOP FIGHTING!"

Sudden silence. Everyone turned to her in surprise. The only sound was a click-click-clicking. Willa turned to see Mab in the parlour, eagerly taking in all the action from the dollhouse roof as she knitted, her scarf hanging halfway down to the floor. Willa cleared her throat.

"I need to tell all of you about Horace's augury...."

Belle interrupted with a snort. "Augury. What a load of garbage!"

Willa's attention was suddenly caught by a black spot trickling darkness down the wall. She spun around to glare up the stairs at Belle.

"BELLE! Fighting makes the spots worse! Can't you see that?"

Silence. Willa looked around at them all, at the end of her rope. "I am sick and tired of everyone arguing all the time!" She jabbed a finger at the stain on the wall. "This ... is ... serious! Just listen, will you?"

Belle sat back, too surprised to sulk. Instead she eyed the dark stain and kept quiet. Willa took another breath and continued, outlining quickly what Horace had told her earlier. She let everyone take it in for a moment before going on.

"I'm pretty sure everything he saw is true. I mean, look at the blackness everywhere. And the birds out there. Where did they come from?"

"Butcher birds," offered Horace. "Nasty, pestilential things. They're not from the Other Side, but they tend to show up wherever dark forces are gathering."

Willa began to pace, her mind racing. "So the dark spots are signs that ... something ... is coming. And the birds are another sign. We don't know who is coming, or what, or why, but it's definitely bad news. Right?"

Everyone nodded silently. From the darkness at the top of the stairs Belle spoke up, her voice softer, more fearful. "We've got to call Miss Trang."

"She's conferring with the Grand Council," said Horace. "They'll need to hear about this as well. I'm sure they have no idea … I'll … I'll call her." But as he started up the stairs there was a sudden sharp thud.

"The office," mouthed Willa, pointing to the door. Everyone gathered behind her as she gingerly took hold of the doorknob. Steeling herself, she swung the door open.

The room was upside down, desk drawers scattered about, papers, files, and books all over the floor. In the middle of the mess three black cats were feverishly searching through it all. The creatures spun to face them. Willa was shocked to see they had human faces, with enormous black eyes growing larger and larger. They withdrew their weird long fingers from the papers and advanced, arching their backs and hissing.

Baz was the first to react. She pushed her way past Willa and pounced on the nearest cat with a shriek. The other two quickly fell back, scrambling toward the far wall, which was peppered with holes and torn wallpaper. As they escaped into the wall there was a sudden loud skittering noise and spiders began pouring out of the holes, large, gangly creatures with eight-inch legs. With a fearful clattering they quickly covered the walls, ceiling, and floor.

Willa pulled back in terror, but Robert let out a great roar and pushed through them to enter the room. He thundered around, trampling the insects with heavy hooves. Everything shook.

Tengu followed next, howling and stomping. Mab buzzed in swinging a straightpin sword, which she thrust into the nearest spider. Horace thwacked at them with the fireplace shovel.

Willa armed herself with an ornate doorstop from the hall and began slamming it down on one insect after another. They crumpled, their legs crimping like wires.

Belle held the last line of defence in the hallway, wheeling deftly over any insects that tried to escape the office.

The combined offensive held the spiders back, but only just. A loud clanging sounded in the living room and Willa ran in to find Fadiyah crashing wildly into the bars of her cage. Willa opened the cage door, and in a flash of gold and red the bird joined the others in the office, screaming and ripping the spiders apart with her claws and bill.

The scene was absolute chaos. Tengu climbed the upended furniture to dive into the fray. The golden bird razed through the insects on the ceiling, ripping them apart and tossing the pieces aside. The birds outside thumped into the windows, threatening to break the glass. Robert swung around, hip-checking Baz into the corner. Willa ran to help her. A cut over one eye was bleeding profusely but she just grinned and got back to work.

Finally it was over. Dead spiders littered the floor as the last few living ones fled, disappearing back into the holes.

Robert leaned against the desk, breathing heavily but beaming. He roared with laughter. "Those little beggars will think twice about coming back!"

Tengu sat on the floor, panting. Willa was out of breath too and shivering uncontrollably. The golden bird landed suddenly in front of her, startling her, and looked deeply into her eyes. Willa felt calmer, and found her voice.

"Is everyone all right?"

Baz crouched in a corner with a spider in her mouth, which she shook furiously.

"Oh, for goodness sake, Baz. Drop it. Drop it!" barked Belle from the hall. Baz reluctantly let the spider fall. Blood was still dripping from the cut on her head.

Willa looked around anxiously. "Where's Mab?"

They found her weakly trying to free herself from a spider web over the doorway. Robert reached up and gently pulled her free, passing her down to Willa. Willa stared at the tiny form in her hand, uncertain about what to do. Mab gestured and Willa leaned her ear close.

"Keep my scarf safe," Mab whispered. "Keep it safe!"

"I will, I promise," answered Willa with a smile.

They returned her to the dollhouse. Willa tucked her into bed, uncertain of what else could be done. She gathered the knitting needles and silvery scarf from where they'd been dropped and tucked them under the fairy's bed.

Mab let out a wheezy cough and fell into a deep sleep. Willa felt sick at heart.

"I will call Miss Trang," Horace announced and started slowly up the stairs. Willa watched him go, her fingers crossed.

"You can do it, Horace. I know you can," she said softly.

In the parlour the others were all talking at once. The action seemed to have aroused everyone's fighting spirit. Robert crowed about their victory and Tengu hopped about grinning and cheering. Belle was flushed and bright-eyed but cautious.

"It isn't over yet. Not by a long shot," she ventured, and Willa felt inclined to agree.

Belle was struggling to tie a hastily made cardboard cone around Baz's head while the old lady hissed and tried to pull away from her.

"It's for your own good," chuckled Belle. "If you keep scratching at it the cut will never heal." The sight of Baz sulking in her cone cheered Belle up considerably.

Willa dropped wearily onto the couch. "Those cats, or whatever they were, were looking for something. What could they want?" No one had an answer.

"All right, we've got to get ready for whatever's coming next. We need to marshal our forces." Willa looked around the room. "Aren't all of you magic in some way? What kind of spells can you do?"

"We're retired, dearie," explained Belle, as the others exchanged embarrassed looks. "Have been for a long ... LONG time. It was a rule of this place not to go exercising magic willy-nilly all over the place. You can't expect us to remember anything useful now." To Willa's dismay this seemed to be the general consensus.

"Oh, come on now! You're always bragging about charms and spells and things ... all of you. There must be some kind of magic you can do here," she appealed.

Tengu was scratching his head. "Hand-to-hand, mortal combat is more my thing. EeYAWWW!" He struck a pose, fists cocked. From behind Belle whacked him in the head with a sofa cushion and he retreated in a sulk.

Willa peeked into the cone. "Baz? Please. Anything at all."

"I know a million spells," exclaimed Baz, her face lighting up. "Let me see now ... curdling milk, straightening curls, opening locked doors, clouding clear waters, removing stains, curing bunions, turning wine into water ..."

"What?!" exclaimed Robert, aghast. "Reprehensible!"

Baz went on. "I know how to make someone's hair fall out. I can give someone the hiccups. I can make toast fall with the buttered side *up*."

"You know a million *useless* spells," Robert snorted. Baz fixed an angry eye on him.

"Okay, Robert. What about you then?" Willa turned hopefully to the centaur.

"I don't deal in silly little spells — *hic!*" Robert frowned. "My charms and incantations are more serious in natur — *HIC!*" He stomped a hoof. "HIC! Baz! HIC! Undo this. HIC! ImmediateHIC!"

Tengu giggled wildly. Baz rolled her eyes and snapped her fingers. Robert breathed easily again.

"You were saying," Willa prompted.

"I was saying that my particular skills involve bigger things ... forces of nature and whatnot."

"For example?"

Here Robert looked a little less certain. "Err ... lights at night, the nocturnal proclivities of woodland animals, rainbows, bird migration, phases of the moon ..."

"You can control the phases of the moon?"

"Control? No. Not as such." Robert frowned. "But knots in a rope can change the weather."

"Only rope braided from unicorn hair," corrected Baz. Robert nodded sadly.

"A nail in the pocket guards against pixies," offered Tengu. "But I suppose that doesn't help us much."

"Not really." Willa turned to Belle, who was being unusually quiet. "What about you, Belle? What can you do?"

But the mermaid just stared at the floor, she wouldn't meet Willa's gaze. "Nothing specific. Curses. But I don't do them anymore."

Willa shook her head. This was getting them nowhere. "Come on," she sighed. "Let's try to block up the holes in the office."

They got to work moving the desk and bookshelves against the wall full of holes. As they worked, Willa peered out the window. She saw no sign of the butcher birds, but the fog was so thick she couldn't be sure they were gone. Once the wall was adequately barricaded they couldn't think of anything else to do, so everyone headed up for bed.

Willa took the first shift keeping watch. She wandered nervously around the house. She listened at the library door to Horace mumbling and pacing. For a long while she stared in at Mab, who seemed to be resting all right.

Willa stood on the back steps and breathed in the night air. The yard was dark and silent, no sign of butcher birds. It was so still it was hard to believe what had just happened in the house. She tiptoed through the misty yard toward Dinah, feeling guilty about forgetting her in all the excitement.

Dinah was awake, which was pretty unusual. Willa foraged around for greenery to feed her but she didn't seem interested in food, which was also pretty unusual. Dinah seemed anxious, snuffling at Willa and trying to put her head under her hands. Willa finally stopped and gently stroked her neck. The dinosaur blinked at her questioningly, so Willa told her what had happened.

"They come out of the walls, and we're not sure when they'll come again. I think we'll be all right, but I'm not totally sure."

Dinah hung her head so heavily, it nearly knocked Willa over. Willa looked her straight in one big eye.

"Would you like to help us fight them?"

Slowly, the great head moved up and down slightly. Willa held her breath. She'd never before felt that Dinah could understand her words.

"Thank you," she whispered.

Dinah slowly swung her head away. Shuffling her feet awkwardly, she lay down again with a heavy thump and a wheeze. Willa turned away, thinking sadly that the dinosaur would probably not be able to put up much of a fight, no matter how willing she was.

Of course that goes for all of us, she thought glumly.

On the way back to the house Willa suddenly remembered the tree nymphs. They too were aware that something was amiss. As Willa tiptoed through the foggy trees, they gathered around her, their voices chittering softly.

As she began speaking they fell silent. Again she explained what had happened. To her surprise they just stared blankly at her, heads cocked as if to say "so?" She tried again, her anxiety rising.

"The Dark Forces will come back! They'll take over the house! And ... the world, and everything! Don't you even care?"

The fairies blinked and exchanged looks. "No" seemed to be the consensus. Willa could not believe what she was seeing. She glared at them angrily.

"Fine. They'll probably cut your trees down for kindling. Then we'll see if you care or not!"

Furious, she stomped away, but there was a sudden uproar behind her, a buzzing like an upended wasp's nest. She turned back to see the reaction she was hoping for. The fairies were hopping up and down, raising their tiny fists and ready for a fight.

Willa wandered aimlessly about the silent house for hours. At three o'clock it was time to wake Robert for the next shift. Before going upstairs, however, she decided to take a last look at the office.

Doorstop in hand, she tiptoed into the room and peeked behind the desk. Thankfully, the holes in the wall didn't seem to have grown any larger, but something glinted in the darkness. Heart pounding, she inched closer, crouching to peer through one of the larger openings. In the dense black beyond the wall something shifted. Something large, glistening, and black. A grey eye twitched open, and Willa stumbled back and fled from the room.

hapter Twelve

Time runs out

Willa woke again and again through the night, her mind cloudy and confused. It was a familiar feeling. Since Mab was out of commission, they'd be getting no dreams again, and everyone would be tired and irritable.

Great, thought Willa. *That's just what we need right now.*

When she finally opened her eyes to the morning light, everything was quiet. She arose and dressed quickly. Outside, all was grey and woolly. Instead of burning off in the light of the rising sun, the fog had grown thicker. Willa could barely make out the shapes of the houses across the street. As she slipped on her shoes a loud thump and crash reverberated through the house.

Another crash as she hit the hallway. The noise was coming from the library. She sprinted down the hall and threw open the door.

Horace was angrily flinging books across the room. Willa glanced about wildly but saw nothing.

"Horace! Horace! What is it?"

Horace turned to her, his features twisted in frustration and rage. "I can't ... I can't ..." The anger drained suddenly from his face, and he fell into an armchair, covering his face with his hands. In the sudden silence came a strange sound ... sobbing. Horace's shoulders shook. Willa ran and put her arm around him.

"Horace, please. What's wrong?"

Horace raised his face from his hands and looked up at her with a look of total despair. I ... I can't do it," he rasped, his voice nearly gone. "I can't call Miss Trang. I tried but I ... I ..." He gestured helplessly.

Robert appeared in the doorway, armed with a fireplace poker. He scanned the room, ready for a fight.

"Where are they? Just point me at 'em and I'll ..."

Horace rose, his cheeks still wet with tears. "I'm the enemy here, my friend." He turned back to Willa. "In my youth I could have summoned her like that!" He snapped his fingers. "I could do it in my sleep. And now ..." He sagged, looking old and defeated. His voice was a hoarse whisper. "I can't remember the words. I have them and then they're gone. There are days I can't even remember who I am."

He sank back into his chair. Robert blinked in surprise and backed quietly out of the room. Willa put her arms around Horace's shoulders.

"It's all right," she cooed, as if she were talking to a small child. "We'll figure this out. We'll manage, don't worry...." But her heart was sinking ever lower as she spoke the words.

She helped Horace to his room. He fell asleep as soon as he lay down and Willa went downstairs. She felt totally disjointed and jumpy; she had no idea what would happen next.

Another house meeting convened in the dining room, without Horace.

"Horace couldn't call Miss Trang," Willa said simply, not wanting to say any more than that. As she feared, Belle started grousing right away.

"Well, we should have seen that coming. Mr. Know-it-All can't deliver, eh?"

It was decided that since Miss Trang could not be summoned, someone had to go directly to the Grand Council and find her. Robert knew the way and could certainly travel the quickest of any of them, so he was selected for the job.

Half an hour later, hearty goodbyes were exchanged as Robert clip-clopped out the front door and picked his way down the porch steps. Willa looked up and down nervously. She had no idea how he would do this without being seen. It was still early, though, the streets were empty and the fog grew ever thicker. In fact, visibility was now so bad that Willa couldn't see the houses across the street at all.

She walked with Robert to the front gate. The air was calm and cold. Nothing moved. As Willa slung a bag of provisions around his neck, Robert smiled at her.

"No problem. I'll fetch Miss Trang as quick as a wink and she'll take care of all this nonsense. She's more ... *up* on this sort of thing than we are. You'll see."

He was trying to reassure her, but as Willa looked up at him she knew they were both frightened.

"I know, Robert. We'll be okay." She gave him a warm smile and he trotted off into the fog with a final salute.

Back inside Willa found Horace coming down the stairs, very slowly, his white hair sticking out in all directions. She offered her arm and he leaned on it heavily.

"Robert's gone to bring Miss Trang back."

Horace just nodded, not meeting her eyes. She led him toward the parlour, where great whallops and thuds could be heard.

Tengu was teaching Belle and Baz some kind of martial art. All three were armed with mop and broom handles, the ends whittled into crude spears. They were whipping these homemade weapons around in a menacing fashion. Menacing to the china, mostly, as the occasional teacup was dispatched with a musical crash. Baz in particular was having great difficulties, since the cone around her neck was seriously hampering her vision.

Willa called for a halt. The threesome grinned at each other, obviously quite proud of themselves and feeling quite dangerous.

"What I wouldn't give for a good war hammer right now," sighed Tengu. "Then nothing could stop us!"

He struck a warlike pose. Willa just smiled. Horace

settled into his favourite armchair. Willa looked in on Mab. She still lay in a deep sleep. The needles and yarn were under her bed. Willa plunked down on the sofa and looked at them all.

"Why is all this even happening? I don't get it. Why is the Other Side coming *here*? What do they want from all of you?"

"It's not about us," Belle answered, shaking her head. "We are of no use to anyone anymore."

"Then what do they want? We have to figure this out or we can't fight them. *What do they want?*"

Tengu shrugged. "They've always wanted to live in this world."

"So what's stopping them?"

"Time."

Willa turned. It was Horace, staring at the floor as if in a trance. "Our 'eternal world' time is different from your 'mortal world' time. The only way we can live in your world is if we monitor our time to move along at the same pace as yours. The Other Side has never been able to do this."

"And how do you do it?"

Horace shook his head. "Oh, *I* don't do it. I'm afraid I've never paid much attention to such things. Miss Trang's responsibility, you know. This house must have a talisman of some sort, with some kind of action that regulates the time — keeps our time in here the same as the time out there."

Willa thought hard. "A talisman ... that must be what the cats were looking for. Does anyone know what our talisman is?" She looked to the others but they all shrugged. "So how do we know they haven't got it yet?"

"If the Other Side had it we would certainly know." Horace was sitting straighter in his chair. He was starting to sound like his old self, speaking with more authority. "For one thing we would all be destroyed, and probably the town as well. The Dark Forces would use the talisman to enter the mortal world, existing in proper time with it, and thus be able to conquer it."

Horace looked a little superior for a moment. "After all, you humans don't have anything that would be useful in fighting the Dark Forces. Nothing that would do much good at all."

This made Willa feel rather cold inside, but she tried to stay on track. "So they don't have it. But they are coming for it. Coming in through the holes in the walls to look for it. And we have to protect it and keep it safe ... but we don't even know what it is!"

Willa shook her head. The situation seemed hopeless, but the challenge seemed to have roused Horace. He rose from his chair and headed toward the office, a new life in him, new strength in his voice. "Don't look so glum, my dear. Let's apply a little brainpower to the problem."

They all set to work searching for the talisman, without any idea of what it was. Willa didn't know how they'd know when they found it, but the others were eager. In fact, they were more energetic and cheerful than she'd ever seen them. As a group they combed through the mess of Miss Trang's office, then headed upstairs to her room.

At the door Willa felt the others hesitate, hanging back fearfully. Willa had never been allowed inside, and obviously they'd never gone in either. She gave them a smile. "She's not here, remember," she said and reached for the doorknob.

Miss Trang's room was actually very easy to search, because there was nothing in it. It was a large room with a high vaulted ceiling, but there wasn't a stick of furniture. Not even a bed. They looked around in some confusion.

"She doesn't sleep," whispered Baz in awe.

"Not in a bed at least," muttered Horace, nervously glancing up at the rafters.

Their search grew quieter and more urgent as they progressed through every room in the house, ending up back in the parlour. They sat and were silent for a long while. Finally Belle cleared her throat.

"It's quiet in here. Too quiet."

"No knitting needles clicking away," said Willa with a smile. Their eyes fell on the dollhouse.

"I always take my naps here, listening to Mab knitting," said Baz, her voice soft with worry. "I mean ... I used to. Clickety clickety clickety ..."

Belle rolled her eyes. "Clickety clack all day. She's been knitting that same scarf ever since I moved in here, and never finishes it!"

Willa sat up suddenly. "Horace, you said earlier that a time talisman required some kind of action?"

"Yes, some kind of movement is needed. I knew of a kettle talisman once. It had to be kept boiling at all times. Someone had to pour water into it constantly." Horace paused, smiling. "The humidity turned the place into a steambath. Curled all the wallpaper."

Tengu spoke up. "I heard of a house where the residents had a deck of cards for a talisman. They had to keep playing gin rummy or time would stop. They had shifts of three hours on, three hours off, all day and all night ..."

Willa wasn't listening. She was down on her knees at the dollhouse. She pulled out a tiny bundle of loose yarn which she held it up triumphantly, her eyes bright.

"The scarf!" she crowed.

Belle sniffed. "That's not a scarf, that's yarn."

"It's yarn now, but it *was* a scarf." Willa appealed to Horace. "When I first saw this it was about eight inches long. During our meeting last night it was only five or six inches long. When we put her to bed I noticed some of it had unravelled. And now it's unravelled even more. Isn't it possible that Mab's *knitting* was keeping our time going?"

A smile slowly spread over Horace's face. "Willa, you're a wonder!"

Willa turned back to the dollhouse, suddenly very conscious of the single strand of yarn running back into Mab's bedroom. She followed it carefully to the needles. There were only a few rows of knitting left. As they all stared, the stitches ever so slowly dropped out, like an invisible hand was tugging at the yarn. Willa's eyes grew wide.

"Our time is running out!" She looked around. "Does anyone know how to knit?"

Head shakes, panicky looks. Willa stared helplessly at the tiny needles in her hand, smaller than toothpicks. Why had she never learned to knit? Her mother had offered to teach her once, she remembered, and a sudden wave of despair swept over her.

She shut her eyes, wishing her mom was there. She heard nothing but wind for a moment, and felt cold. Then in her mind she could see her mom knitting, patiently clicking away at a green toque. Willa tried to focus on her hands. She could see them in action, looping the yarn around, tucking it under....

When she opened her eyes the needles were still in her palm, with only one row of tiny stitches in place.

"Get me a magnifying glass!" she hollered, dropping to her knees and trying to get a grip on the needles with her big, clumsy fingers. Horace raced into the office and came back with the glass. He tried to hold it over the knitting, but his hand shook so much that he had to give it to Belle, who was steady as a rock.

"Go on, Willa," she urged, her voice firm.

Willa looped and tucked once, twice, slowly getting into the swing of it, but her stitches were big and uneven next to Mab's fine work, which was nearly all gone now. She paused, just for a moment, as the last of the tiny stitches was pulled by that unseen hand. Horace moved to the window and peered out.

ﾭ8m

ﾭ8m

"We're still in time, but it's ... clunky."

Willa squinted and hurriedly knitted two full rows of crazy stitches, then jumped up to look out the window.

The fog had thinned somewhat. The butcher birds lined the fence again, and beyond that a few neighbours were out on the street. She saw immediately what Horace meant by "clunky." People were moving jerkily, fast for a moment, then slow, fast, slow, then infinitely slow. And the daylight flickered like an old-fashioned silent movie, cold and grey.

"It's my knitting," wailed Willa. "My hands are too big!" Then she saw a familiar figure a little distance down the road.

"MOM!"

Her mother was dashing, in slow motion, toward the house. She was in her bathrobe, with her hair in disarray and slippers flapping under her feet. Everyone else on the street seemed in a trance but her mom's face was full of panic and concern. She was coming to them, to help! Willa choked back a sob, excited and hopeful. Then she looked down to her knitting again. She had to knit enough time for her mom to get there.

She stared down at her work. She could hardly hear the others, they seemed far away, indistinct. She tried to keep knitting, but her hands were shaking now and her heart was pounding.

"Horace! What will happen if I stop?"

Horace's voice burbled quietly but she could make out none of the words. Even the click of the needles was muffled now, but she was too scared to look up. She was shaking so bad she could barely continue, and her stitches were getting worse. She heard a scream and the screeching of birds. She looked up.

Her mom was at the front gate. The butcher birds were in the air, circling, their talons extended as they swiped murderously at her. She slowed and shielded her face with her arms, but the birds tore at her sleeve. They swooped and she stumbled, grabbing on to the fence for support. The largest butcher bird dove at her, its claws aimed at her exposed face.

Willa let out a cry as she grabbed the loose end of the yarn and yanked out all of her stitches. She caught a brief glimpse of the bird, frozen in place in the air, of her mother cowering ... then there was a great cracking sound, like very sharp thunder. The air seemed to shatter, the light outside exploded, white and blinding. Then all was still.

Time had stopped. And they were alone.

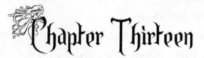

Chapter Thirteen

Them and It

Willa squeezed her eyes closed against the painfully bright light, squeezing the tiny ball of yarn in her fist. After a few moments the light began to dim and she could hear the others moving about. Willa cautiously opened her eyes. They were all still there. The parlour was still there. Out the window she could see the yard up to the gate, but beyond that was a blank grey page. It wasn't foggy grey, but flat grey, like a painted wall. Willa could make out a few of the butcher birds in frozen poses in the air but couldn't see her mother at all. Beyond the gate and fence there was nothing.

Horace, Belle, Baz, Tengu, and Willa looked at each other in the pale light. Behind them was a faint, incessant clanging as Fadiyah restlessly circled her cage.

Horace cleared his throat. "We are now outside time."

The others sat down. Willa stood alone in the middle of the room. "Are we ... in *your* time?" her voice trembled. "Magic time? Immortal time?"

"No, unfortunately."

"We're someplace else entirely?"

"Some*time* else, yes."

Willa sighed. She sensed that thinking too hard about this time business would just get in the way of what had to be done.

"So we are all alone?" she persisted. Horace nodded and she went on. "Can the *other* side find us here?"

Horace nodded again. "Oh, yes. We're even closer to them now."

Willa pointed out at the blank greyness. "What if we went out there. Went somewhere else?"

Horace gazed out the window, squinting doubtfully. "There's nowhere else out there. I don't know what *is* there, but if we go through that gate we might never find our way back, and this house is the only way to get back to your world."

He started, turning back. "They're coming. Listen."

There was a faint skittering sound in the walls, and the creaking of boards, as if the house was shifting on its foundation. Then the sound of fabric tearing. Willa felt jittery.

"Everyone! Get ready!"

Tengu jumped to his feet and gathered up the broom handles. Belle removed the cone from around Baz's neck.

"Now don't go scratching at your cuts," Belle scolded. "Or I'll put it right back on." Baz scowled but said nothing. Tengu held out their mop handle weapons.

"We're not going to get far with sticks, Tengu," grumbled Belle.

The golden bird hopped about urgently, making the cage jump and clang on its stand. Willa opened the cage door and Fadi stepped out onto her arm.

"You know something's about to happen, don't you?" Willa cooed softly, smoothing the bird's feathers. Calmed, Fadi looked into Willa's eyes, tilted her head and nodded. Then she hopped onto the back of the sofa and stretched her glittering wings out to the sides.

Willa put her ear to the office door. The sounds were growing louder in there, with the addition of the stealthy scrape of something very, very large. She turned to Horace again, whispering.

"The knitting needles are the time talisman. We've just got to keep them hidden, right?"

"Yes," Horace nodded. "If they don't have the needles they cannot enter and live in your world. And we can always get back in time by starting to knit again."

Willa nodded and opened her palm. She let out a gasp. Only the ball of yarn was there. She dashed back into the parlour and dropped to her knees, groping frantically for the tiny needles on the rug. Horace stumbled in behind her, dropping down as well and fumbling about.

A loud crash sounded in the office. Fadiyah flew out of the room with Tengu close behind, spinning his mop handle artfully. Baz fumbled for her broomstick and followed. Belle wheeled herself out, her pale fingers clenching a fireplace poker.

The noise and shouts grew deafening, but Willa

continued to run her fingers back and forth across the flowered rug, her heart pounding.

"I'll find them, Horace, go!" she yelled. Horace struggled to his feet and dashed out of the room with a roar.

A movement caught Willa's eye. Mab was stirring in her bed. Willa crawled over and gently lifted the fairy, wrapping her in a blanket and slipping her into the inner pocket of her jacket. Then a horrifying scream from Belle made her jump.

The old lady had slipped out of her chair at the foot of the stairs, screaming more in anger than fear as she swung her poker at three cat-people who hissed and reared up to pounce.

Willa grabbed a cushion from the sofa and ran out into the hall. She started to whack the cats as hard as she could. They tumbled backwards and scampered back into the office.

"I could have handled those furballs," grumbled Belle as Willa helped her into the wheelchair.

"I know, but I need you in here." Willa wheeled her into the parlour doorway. "Try to keep the cats out of here. The needles are still in the rug somewhere."

She expected an argument from the old woman, but Belle nodded purposefully and pointed to the pillow Willa still had in her hand.

"A pillow's not going to cut it, sweetie. Here!" Belle held out her poker.

"No, you keep it." Willa tossed the pillow aside and grabbed the fireplace shovel.

The scene in the office was fierce. The far wall was one great empty black hole now and the lithe cat-people were slithering in, swarming the place despite the tremendous efforts of Horace, Baz, and Tengu. Horace was in lion form, big and golden, pouncing on the cats with a great roar, clawing and flinging them across the room. Baz was fighting fire with fire, hissing and swiping with her claws. Fadi swooped back and forth, scattering the felines. The most amazing sight, however, was Tengu, flashing around the room in a blur, forward, backward, spinning and flipping. His mop handle whooshed back and forth with eerie precision, cracking cat spines with every blow. The cats were falling and being thrown, but they kept coming.

"Horace!" called Willa. "There's too many of them!"

The lion paused, nodding his great head, and backed into the doorway of the office, effectively blocking it.

"Stand back!" he roared. Tengu, Baz, and Willa shrank back into the corners of the room. The bird perched above the window. The cats, suddenly silent, turned to stare at Horace in the doorway.

In the sudden quiet Willa could hear Horace mumbling, menace in his voice. Then he roared and swiped with his paw, creating a visible disturbance in the air. It spread outward in a semi-circle, like ripples in a lake, and the cats were blown back by the shock-wave. They flew back into the hole or thunked against the wall, dropping to the floor. Then they sprang as one at Horace, like a wave splashing back at him, but he

144

waved his paw again, in a wide, strong sweep, and the cats were thrown back with even greater force. Many fell unconscious to the floor, but still more cats poured out of the wall.

Horace was hanging his head wearily now as the cats crept forward, slowly covering the whole floor. He braced himself in the frame of the doorway as they began to climb all over him, mewling terribly.

The bird flapped back and forth, screeching angrily, diving and tearing at their backs, but the cats paid it no mind. Tengu, Baz, and Willa leapt back into the fray but it was a losing battle. They couldn't even get close to Horace, who was sinking into an ocean of cats.

"Horace!" screamed Willa as he disappeared from sight. Just then the room seemed to explode behind her. Shards of glass filled the air and Willa fell forward, landing on cats. The next moment she was beneath them. She couldn't breathe. Their feet scratched and scrambled over her. When she felt an opening she rolled over and sat up. A large, dark shape loomed above her. And a large, moist eye.

Dinah let out an ear-splitting wail as the last of the cats slipped away into the darkness beyond the wall. Willa and the others sat up on the glass-strewn floor exchanging looks of amazement. Dinah had thrust her head through the window, sending the terrified cats into retreat. Now she closed her eyes and let out a tremendous cry of victory. The sound reverberated for a long time through the still house.

"Dinah! Thank you, thank you!" Willa threw her

arms around the dinosaur's neck. The others gathered around with happy shouts and hugs, and Dinah closed her eyes, snuffling humbly.

Willa looked to Horace, small and human again, slumped in the doorway. His face and hands were criss-crossed with bright red scratches. She ran over to help him up.

"Horace, are you okay?" He was too breathless to answer but waved her aside, standing on his own.

The office was in a shambles, but more than that, the black stains and puddles had multiplied all over the room, scattered around like spattered paint. Pulsating. Silently everyone stepped around them, withdrawing from the office into the narrow hallway. Belle was out of her chair, sitting on the floor in the parlour, wide-eyed. "What happened?"

"Dinah happened, that's what," cackled Baz. Belle grinned as they helped her back into her chair.

Willa caught her breath. "She surprised them, but they'll be back. The hole's too big to block now, we'll have to barricade the doorway!"

Tengu jumped to the stairs and braced his mop handle against the bannister, which gave way and splin-tered apart, trailing ragged nails. He and Baz hurriedly hammered scraps of wood across the office doorway. Horace seemed totally exhausted; he sat on the stairs and watched silently.

Willa turned to the parlour. Belle was looking very pleased with herself.

"No need to look. I found them," she crowed.

"Belle! That's fantastic!" Willa gave her an impulsive hug and felt the bony shoulders melt a little. She held out her hand for the needles but Belle shook her head.

"No, no. I'll look after them."

Willa felt her face growing hot. "Belle! We don't have time to argue!"

"So stop arguing!"

"Give them to me right now!"

Willa surprised herself. She sounded like her mom. She was talking to Belle as if the mermaid were a small child. She felt a twinge of guilt. Belle was staring back at her in that I'm-not-to-be-meddled-with way.

"I may be old and I may be foolish, but I am *not* totally useless!"

Willa still felt she was in the right. *She* was the one to safeguard the needles, but there was no way to get them, short of strong-arming an old woman in a wheelchair, and she wasn't about to do that.

"All right," she sighed. "Where do you have them?"

Belle's hand slipped into her sweater pocket. Willa just nodded and turned away.

The office doorway was haphazardly boarded up now. Everyone stepped back to wait.

Willa headed out the back door and hurried into the trees. The fairies were all about, sitting in branches and armed with slivers of spears, or bows and arrows. Willa pulled Mab from her pocket, stirring and newly awake. Willa breathed a sigh of relief as Mab blinked, trying weakly to sit up. The fairies scowled at the sight of her, but Willa would have none of it.

147

"I don't care if you've got some stupid old feud with her. She needs your help right now! We could lose everything here, you've GOT to do the right thing!"

Willa felt the desperation in her voice, but she was so forceful that the fairies paused, exchanging looks. Then they directed Willa to a hollow in a tree. She lay Mab down and watched as they covered her up with leaves and feathers.

"Thank you," Willa called back as she hurried off.

Next Willa went to see Dinah. The dinosaur's chin rested on the windowsill and she eyed the office warily. Willa suddenly felt tired, very tired. She leaned against Dinah, closing her eyes for a moment. All was silent. Nothing moved. There was no breeze, no air. It was as if her ears were plugged with cotton. Willa squeezed her eyes shut, enjoying the silence and willing it to continue. It didn't.

There was a strange whooshing sound next, like an underground river, and a breeze hit her.

She opened her eyes. The black hole was now bulging into the office, like a great black bubble of nothing about to burst into the room. As Willa and Dinah stared, the bubble wobbled and snapped, and darkness flowed into the room.

When the thick black liquid had covered the floor it began to pull together and solidify. A form took shape, long and snake-like, but huge. The tail end disappeared into the black hole. The front end swung back and forth. The face was blank, featureless. Then, as Willa stared, a mouth ripped open and a barbed black tongue snapped out, whipping around the room. Searching. The massive beast filled the room, thrashing its tongue back and forth like a blind man's cane.

Unable to move or even breathe, Willa watched. How could they fight *that?*

Chapter Fourteen

The Mouth

The great black snake scraped across the office. Cats and spiders spilled out of its mouth. The cats spread over the floor and the spiders covered the walls and ceiling, turning the entire room black. Dinah thrust her head in, bellowing. The spiders skittered, the cats backed away, but the snake paid no attention.

Willa dashed to the back door, nearly tripping over the two-headed lizard fleeing the house to disappear in the long grass. Inside she found the old folks staring at the office door as Dinah's roaring sounded from within.

"Get back!" hollered Willa, running up. "Get away from the door!"

They were just beginning to move when the office door exploded into pieces around them. Tengu and Baz fell toward the front door, Belle and Horace to the stairs. The dark shape flowed through them into the parlour, a rippling blackness six feet high blocking the hallway. Tengu and Baz disappeared outside. Horace stood halfway up the stairs in total shock. Belle's wheelchair had tipped over at the foot of the stairs, where she lay, her face agape in horror.

The cats and spiders appeared next. The spiders streamed across the ceiling. The cats scrambled over the back of the seemingly endless form of the snake, grinning evilly. Willa scrambled over the broken bannister onto the stairs.

"Get upstairs, Horace! We're right behind you!" She slid her hands under Belle's arms and dragged her out of the fallen chair. It sounded like the parlour was being smashed to dust.

Willa inched her way backwards, heaving Belle up the stairs, step by step. The cats swarmed over the empty chair and dropped onto Belle's tail, which she swung back and forth energetically, sweeping them off the stairs but causing Willa to stumble. She struggled to keep a grip on Belle and nearly dropped her again when she backed into Horace.

"Horace! Move!" Willa looked back over her shoulder. Her blood froze. His face was blank and confused, his eyes darting about.

"Have you ... have you seen my glasses? I seem to have misplaced them," he stammered. Above them spiders rushed over the ceiling, heading to the second floor ahead of them.

"They're in the library, old man. MOVE IT!" hollered Belle.

Horace blinked and retreated up the stairs. The noise in the parlour suddenly abated. The thing glinted in the dim light, retracting. Willa heaved and tugged Belle up the stairs, slipping and stumbling with every step.

The snakehead pulled back into the hallway. Belle gasped. The cats withdrew silently as the head swung over to the stairs. The mouth gaped open toward them. Willa held her breath. The interior of the thing went on and on forever, and there were shapes in there, voices, howling wind, and great cold space. There was a whole universe inside, just waiting to come out.

Then the tongue snapped out, slapping and bumping up the stairs. They both shrieked, their cries lost in the screech of the golden bird, diving at the tongue with claws outstretched. One talon thunked into a stair, but the tongue had simply split in two to escape being impaled; now two tongues whipped blindly about the stairs. The bird struggled to extract its claw and dodge them.

Willa gave a great lunge backward and sprawled on the second floor landing. She and Belle crawled and scrambled to the library door. There was a sickening thud as Fadi was thrown into a wall behind them.

"Come!" screamed Willa.

Dragging one limp wing, the bird hopped after them into the library and they slammed the door shut.

Willa's breath came in painful gasps; she felt tears flowing down her cheeks. Belle pulled herself across the floor, still gripping her poker, wheezing and cursing as she went. Fadiyah shook herself, stretching her hurt wing and gurgling with great agitation.

Horace sat in an armchair, watching them blankly. Belle opened her mouth, but Willa stopped her.

"He's gone, Belle. There's no use."

Belle said nothing. In the hall they could hear the slither of the tongue and the skitter of cats.

A sudden sharp rap made Willa jump out of her skin. It was Tengu, outside the window. Willa slid the window open.

"May we join you?" he asked cheerfully. He and Baz had come up the fire escape. They tumbled into the room and everyone turned expectantly to Willa. Why did they look to her? She just wanted to fall apart and weep, but something about that swish-swish in the hallway caused her to take a deep breath. She began to pace, mostly to stamp out the shaking in her knees.

"It's like a snake, but it has no eyes," she explained. "It can't see, but its tongue is trying to feel out what it's looking for: the knitting needles. It doesn't care about us, it just wants the needles. And if it gets them ..." She fell silent, at a loss.

Belle thrust one hand into her sweater pocket and brandished her poker with the other. Her face was so pale it looked blue, but her eyes blazed.

"It won't get them," she growled.

In the hall the tongue slapped around, and as they watched, spiders began squeezing in under the door. Baz sprang across the room, pouncing on them. Willa looked around wildly.

"Out the window!"

Tengu jumped forward and slung Belle over his shoulders, fireman-style.

"Aaack! Watch it, you hooligan," she hissed, but

he just grinned and hopped out the window. Willa coaxed Horace to the window. He was like a small, frightened child.

Baz was losing the battle, even though the bird had joined her. The spiders just kept coming. Out in the hall the sound of shattering glass and splintering wood was getting louder. Horace was finally gripping the fire escape ladder and Willa started to follow.

"If anyone has a spell up their sleeves, this would be a good time to pull it out!" she shouted.

Baz gave her a grim nod and turned to face the door. Willa paused on the ladder, watching as the old woman began to mutter and howl weirdly. Then she danced, spinning and hopping to the door and back a few times. Her footprints on the floor glowed in two parallel lines running the length of the room toward the door. There was a loud CRACK and the floor between the lines sagged a little. Baz jumped back, scurrying to the window just as the black head crashed through the library door.

Everyone clambered down the fire escape ladder. Tengu led the way with Belle over his shoulder, then Horace and Willa, and finally Baz. Willa looked up to see tendrils of gossiping hibiscus twining out the window as well.

Somewhere inside the library the bird screeched and the snake's two tongues smashed through the window after them. Glass showered down and the fire escape swung away from the wall. Everyone hung on, shielding their faces. Baz grabbed Willa's arm, her eyes wild with glee.

"Listen! The floor's going!"

Indeed, Willa could hear a great groaning of wood now. The tongues were curving down after them. One flicked sharply at Baz. She swung out of reach, hanging on to the ladder with one hand.

Just then the house, the ladder, the very air vibrated with a tremendous crash. Both tongues zipped back up into the window. Baz cackled crazily as the parlour windows blasted out below their dangling feet.

At the bottom of the ladder Belle slipped from Tengu's grip, but he dove, grabbing hold of her arms and hooking his knees on the bottom rung. They hung there for a moment, like trapeze artists. Then blackness began to ooze out of the broken parlour windows below them.

"Climb up! Climb up!" hollered Tengu, struggling to pull himself and Belle back up.

Horace hugged the ladder, staring at the spiders exiting the library window and covering the front of the house. Willa reached down to tug on his sleeve with her free hand. Baz clambered down the other side of the ladder to grab the old man across the chest and start pulling him up.

"Willa!" screeched Belle.

Willa looked down. Spiders were crawling all over Belle. She was straining, reaching upward with the needles in her hand. Below her blackness filled the yard. Tengu boosted Belle as high as he could, swaying precariously as she handed the needles up to Baz.

Baz grabbed them and swung around to pass them to Willa. As Willa reached for them the ladder swung back against the house with a jolting clang. The needles jumped from her hand. She fumbled, made a last desperate grab. The needles fell.

"NO!"

She stared as they dropped, tiny silver slivers landing on the shiny black back of the beast. The head twisted around and the needles slid off the snake.

Everything fell silent as the tongue ventured out like a dowsing wand, combing back and forth. Willa strained to see. She could just make out a tiny glint on the front walk. She and Belle exchanged frantic looks.

"I'm sorry," Belle mouthed then buried her face in her hands.

Below them the tongue stopped. Willa held her breath, her chest tight. Then the tongue moved on, sliding through the grass in the yard as the beast slithered right past them.

Belle stared up at Willa, who shook her head in amazement. Below them the body of the snake was twining around the corner of the house, the head now out of sight.

"Everybody! Jump down!" Willa called.

Spiders now covered the ladder, but they seemed like the least of their troubles right now. Tengu hung from the bottom rung with one hand, the other arm still wrapped around Belle, and dropped onto the snake's back. They both slid off, landing heavily on the ground. Tengu leaped to his feet, spinning around expectantly, but there was no sign that the snake had even noticed them. Its head was still far out of sight.

The others followed. Willa was the last to slide down from the snake, landing in the grass. Belle was lying on the ground, winded, while the others gazed about them, wide-eyed. Baz dropped to her knees, searching for the needles.

"No, Baz, don't worry about the needles," panted Willa. "It doesn't want them." She looked around. The snake's head was still out of sight. "We need someplace safe ... we need to think...."

"The stable," Tengu ventured. "We can go that way." Willa nodded. Tengu turned toward Belle, who grimaced.

"Here we go again."

Tengu grinned and hoisted her up onto his shoulders once more. The group started off, heading around the corner of the house — the opposite way from where the snake had gone.

Willa brought up the rear, leading Horace. He still looked bewildered and so, so frail. She struggled to get her thoughts straight.

"It doesn't want the needles. But we know for sure that the knitting was regulating our time ... so if the needles weren't doing it ..." She stopped and reached into her pocket. The tiny ball of yarn was still there. "Of course!"

As she gripped the yarn tightly, a gurgling call came from the library above. Willa jumped.

"Fadiyah!"

Chapter Fifteen

The Return

Willa handed Horace over to Baz. "Go on ahead. I'll meet you in the stable!" Then she dashed back, jumping, scrambling up the snake and leaping to grab the ladder.

Willa climbed cautiously into the library. Most of the floor had collapsed into the parlour below. Only fragments remained around the room's perimeter. Clouds of dust hung in the air. The cats had gathered in one corner, surrounding and advancing on the bird. Fadiyah had squeezed into a bookshelf, one wing still hanging awkwardly as she glared and squawked at her attackers.

Willa couldn't get to them. But she grabbed books and pieces of wood, flinging them at the cats until they fell, slipping and tumbling into the hole. Fadiyah hopped painfully across the shelves until Willa could reach and gather her up, whispering and gently smoothing her feathers.

The snake's body still coiled through the library doorway, disappearing down into the parlour. Willa peered down into the hole and saw the cats scrambling over the rubble and out the windows. The parlour was completely destroyed; not a stick of furniture was intact.

Hugging the bird, Willa climbed backwards out the window, but as she felt for the ladder with her foot, something snapped at her ankle. Willa let out a shriek. The head of the snake had doubled back around the house and now the black tongue was flicking up at her. She flung herself and the bird back into the library, nearly falling into the hole. Clutching the bird to her chest, she edged around the room to the door. The black head appeared at the window as she gingerly climbed over its body and out into the hall. She looked back to see the head drop from sight. Where was it going now?

The snake's body took up the entire hallway back to the stairs, down them, and into the office from where it had come. Willa felt certain the thing had no end and would just keep coming and coming after them. Out the smashed hallway windows she could see Tengu leading the others through the overgrown yard to the stable, barely visible through the greenery. The pack of cats rounded the house, dashing toward them. Tengu, Baz, and Belle turned to face them.

Then there was a roar, and to her right she saw Dinah rear up as the snakehead rounded the house. It paused for a moment, then slithered up the wall and across the house, heading straight for the windows ... and Willa!

Willa sprinted down the hallway to the second staircase, and up to her little room. The windows opened to the roof and the fire escape ladder. She might be able to climb down to the ground before the snake realized where she was. But as Willa ran to the nearest window it suddenly turned black. She whirled around. One by one, every window in the circular room went dark, covered by the snake's body.

Behind her the tongue was flapping up the stairs. She dashed about the room in panic. The bird struggled out of her arms, flapping up to perch in the rafters. Willa suddenly remembered there was something that looked like a trapdoor up there, at the peak of the roof. She threw a chair onto her bed and climbed precariously onto it. She heard a slap. The tongue shot across the floor, lashing around a bedpost. It pulled, the bed jerked, and the chair fell. She leaped, grabbing on to a rafter. Pulling herself up, she kicked furiously at the trapdoor. A hot breeze hit the room as the snakehead filled the doorway.

With a last desperate kick, the trapdoor finally came loose and tumbled out of sight. Willa pushed Fadi up through the hole, then followed. She could just barely fit her head and shoulders through the opening.

The roof tiles were damp and cold. Willa could hear shouts from below. She crawled and pulled herself up to look over the peak of the roof into the backyard. Belle lay beside Horace, who seemed to have rallied a bit. He was kicking at the cats as Belle swung her poker. Tengu and Baz were charging the snake from below, stabbing at it with rake and pitchfork. Dinah was sinking her teeth into the snake with no apparent effect.

Suddenly the tongues poked out from the trapdoor. Willa shrieked and scrambled down the roof. There was a tremendous smashing and shaking. The snake's head burst through the roof, its great mouth gulping at the sky. Tiles rained down. Willa slid down the roof, falling. Reaching out blindly, she felt the fire escape ladder and grabbed on.

When she opened her eyes she saw, in a flash, Horace and Belle far below, pointing up at her in horror. She felt a sharp pang of something like regret, and the air was filled with wings and buzzing.

Willa blinked against the light, squinting. Her heart leapt. A host of fairies circled the beast's head. In the lead was Mab, perched in a walnut shell drawn by dragonflies. She sparkled fiercely, her hair snaking out on all sides. She let out the sharpest, highest screech Willa had ever heard.

The snakehead paused, hovering. Mab raised a large shining needle above her head. The fairies flew boldly at the face of the beast. Mab drew back her arm and flung the needle like a spear. It left a shimmering trail as it pierced the lip of the snake. Mab waved her arms like a symphony conductor and the needle zigzagged across the gaping maw, blazing through a lip on each side and leaving in its wake a shimmering golden thread-trail.

Mab was sewing the beast's mouth closed!

Willa clambered down, but her feet soon hit the snake's body, the ladder crushed beneath it. She could do nothing now but hang on.

Mab's needle had travelled across the mouth's expanse once and started back again. The fairies circled, fearlessly pulling on the thread, which tightened slightly, closing the mouth just the tiniest bit. Then the beast snapped out of its reverie and thrashed, flinging fairies all about. It snapped its mouth open wide, shattering the golden line. Mab's chariot fell back and the fairies started to regroup at a distance, but they looked shaken.

Willa glanced down to see Baz and Tengu rejoining Horace and Belle. They were gathering around a large shape. Tengu lifted Belle up onto its back. It was Robert! Robert! Did that mean ... Willa craned around, looking for Miss Trang.

There she was, standing very still in the middle of the yard, hands on hips and gazing calmly up at the snake. Then she lifted a foot and stomped. The ground rumbled beneath her and the house rattled. The snakehead turned toward Miss Trang as she stomped a second time. This time the house jumped on its foundation. From somewhere inside came the sound of breaking glass.

Hanging on tightly, Willa couldn't take her eyes off Miss Trang. She was getting larger, just like that evening in the parlour so long ago. Her hulking shape rose quickly. She was now two storeys tall. Her scowl grew more and more terrible. Willa felt the same cold fear she had felt that night, even though the anger wasn't directed at her this time.

Miss Trang took one last great stomp. Trees toppled. One end of the stable collapsed with a crash. Everyone below dove for cover. Willa stared. Miss Trang's face rose above her like a parade balloon, the features huge, stretched, and distorted. Her face began to rearrange itself. A snout poked out. The skin glittered, hardened into scales. The eyes sunk back in the head, flames leaping within them.

In a few moments the change was complete. Miss Trang stood over the entire scene in her full glory, up on her hind legs, front talons resting on the roof and wings filling the sky. She was an enormous, steely dragon.

With a shattering, raspy cry, the dragon's head darted at the snake. The huge teeth gnashed mere feet above Willa's head. The snake reared back, dodging the dragon's lunges, but it was laced inextricably throughout the house and had little mobility. As it writhed, its body tightened. The house creaked and groaned, its very bones cracking.

The snake coil below Willa tightened too, wrenching the ladder from the roof. Willa screamed, sliding down the roof, picking up speed. She grabbed desperately at roof shingles, but under the pressure of the snake the shingles were popping off and plummeting as well. Willa finally slid into the snake's body and hung on.

Above her Miss Trang and the snake were now partially entwined. The snake had circled once but the dragon had finally sunk its teeth into the snake and began shaking it violently. The massive form thrashed and writhed.

Willa struggled to hang on, wrapping her arms around as much of it as she could. She closed her eyes. Every second she held on might mean that Miss Trang would defeat it. Every second was a second in which she wasn't falling off the roof.

Her thoughts flashed to the tiny ball of yarn, tucked in the inner pocket of her jacket, and as soon as she thought of it she could feel heat radiating from it, warmth right against her heart.

There was a sudden ripping sound very close by. Willa opened her eyes. There was a rip in the snake's body, inches from her face. A long black tear that lengthened, pulling wider and wider. For a brief, glorious moment she wondered if the snake was coming to pieces. Then a black shape moved within, slowly emerging. It was another snakehead, just like the big one, but only a couple of feet across. Its mouth gaped at Willa, advancing on her steadily.

A whooshing sounded in her ears as the air around her was sucked into the maw. Willa backed away, shrieking, but she couldn't hear herself for the rushing air. She felt the yarn burning hot inside her pocket. She swung her body around, kicking viciously at the snake with all her strength. She screamed, roaring at it with every ounce of energy she had left. And kicking, kicking.

The snake wavered for a moment, then snapped its jaws around her foot. Cold shot up her leg, stabbing through her entire body. The yarn was the only point of heat she could feel. She felt numb and unreal as fingers of ice crept through her brain. She kept kicking with her free foot but the snake latched on to it as well. She felt herself slipping, felt her hands slipping as the snake drew her slowly into its mouth. She tried to reach for the yarn in her pocket, thinking to fling it down to the others, but her fingers were frozen and useless.

She glimpsed Miss Trang fighting far above her and tried to call out but no sound came. Her vision became cloudy, sounds muffled. In the fog a shape loomed, hovering over her. She bowed her head, thinking it was another snake ready to finish her off, but the shape emitted a familiar screech. Fadiyah!

The scene snapped back into focus. The bird rose majestically with wings outstretched, though one still hung at a crazy angle. Fadiyah rose without flapping her wings. As the bird ascended above them, all fell silent. Even Miss Trang and the great snake seemed to pause, but all Willa could see was that bird, silhouetted above and looking down at her.

What would it do? What *could* it do?

Fadiyah turned her head to the side, raised her wings even higher, and with a mighty effort swung them down again. It was like lighting a match. The feathers burst into flame as if from the friction of the air. Willa stared in horror, her eyes filling with tears. The flames spread quickly. The bird did not struggle or cry out. The fire bloomed suddenly and Fadiyah disintegrated within it. Gone.

The ball of flame dropped onto the head of the smaller snake, which shrivelled away like a melting plastic bag. Willa pulled her legs free and kicked the burning embers away. The loose shingles smoked and smouldered, and a wall of heat spread across the roof.

Willa slipped off the snake and scrambled down and across the roof, coughing in the smoke. Picking up speed, she slid from the tower roof. Dropping onto the main roof, she kept sliding, farther and faster, but at last out of the heat and smoke. Her feet finally hit the eavestroughing, which bent but held. She looked up.

The fire spread quickly, as if the house had been doused in gasoline. Flames licked up around Miss Trang. The snake was coiled around the tower room, which was now lost in flame. Losing support, the coils collapsed and the snake faltered, dropping in upon itself. Miss Trang leapt upon it then, tearing viciously with tooth and claw. The snake began to withdraw. It retracted, disappearing into and through the house.

Below Willa could see cats and masses of spiders streaming back into the burning house. As the snake withdrew it continued to tighten, squeezing the house. Walls fell. Rooms collapsed. Flames flickered.

The eavestrough below Willa was creaking again, bending precariously. She tried to grab at the shingles but could not get a hold. Her shouts were lost in the roar of the fire.

Above her the dragon lunged furiously at the snake. The two beasts shook the house with their every movement. The eavestrough jittered under Willa's feet until, finally, it snapped.

With a scream Willa dropped onto something, something dry and leathery beneath her fingers. She was on Dinah's snout, staring up into her huge eyes, but before she could breathe a sigh of relief the eyes rolled back in Dinah's head and they both plummeted into the billowing smoke.

Chapter Sixteen

From the ashes

"Willa, honey, it's all right. Everything's all right."

A hand stroked her cheek. Willa groped her way out of the darkness and opened her eyes, squinting at the figure above her.

"Mom?"

In a moment the fuzziness cleared away. It was Belle. Her head was in the mermaid's lap.

"Take it easy, dearie. Dinah broke your fall but you still hit the ground pretty hard."

Willa looked around groggily. Dinah lay nearby, her brow furrowed with concern. Everyone else was there too: Tengu, Baz, Belle, Horace, and Robert with Mab perched on his head. All were bruised, scratched, filthy with soot, and watching her anxiously.

"Willa! Are you all right?"

Willa gently stretched her arms, legs. Sore all over, but ... she nodded and smiled. "I'm okay."

She could see the dragon still standing warily over the burning house. Willa struggled to her feet and ran over just in time to see the one of the office walls cave in. Willa could see into the room now. The wall with the great black hole still stood, with just the head of the snake emerging from it. It flipped back and forth furiously, with the screech of a million voices crying out in pain. The sound knocked her over; it whipped around the yard like a tornado.

As she sat up again, a little dazed, the snakehead turned to her. She froze. The awful noise ceased and the tongue shot out at her. Willa screamed as the remaining office walls caved in and the snake was sucked back into the hole. Bricks, beams, furniture flew through the air, caught up in the whirlwind, then disappeared into the black. The hole seemed to pull itself inside out, finally vanishing with a loud CRACK!

The echoes faded away, the wind died down, and it was all over.

Willa and the dragon locked eyes as the beast shrank back into Miss Trang, small and ordinary in the middle of the yard. Behind her the house continued to burn. Willa became aware of a roaring sound, but it was a reassuring roar, a fireplace kind of roar. Walls continued to fall inward with intermittent crashes. Willa and Miss Trang stared at the blaze.

"The house!" Willa moaned.

Miss Trang shook her head ruefully. "It's not the house that's the problem. I'm more concerned about ..."

She stopped abruptly as her eyes fell on the tiny ball of yarn Willa held out in her hand. Willa had never seen her surprised before. Her eyes grew as large as saucers. The others straggled up and let out a cheer. Miss Trang, in another first, melted into an astonished smile.

"Willa," she gasped. "You are a treasure!"

Just then Baz let out a yelp, pointing at the house. "Look! Up there!" They all turned.

The house still stood, but barely, its walls knock-kneed. In the mass of flames that was once the tower room floated a blinding fireball. At its centre was a small, dark form.

"What is it?" breathed Willa, but no one answered. The form drew itself up and slowly, wings spread out to the sides. Willa gasped. "Is it ... is it Fadiyah?"

Belle grinned. "No, but also yes. In a way."

The small, dark bird, blacker than black, dropped to the roof and hopped unconcernedly through the flames. Reaching the edge of the roof it launched itself, gliding slowly back and forth, zigzagging down to them.

Horace calmly stepped forward, his arm raised. The bird landed on his arm. It was not unlike Fadiyah, but it was a young bird, with an awkward big head and unkempt feathers. Horace gazed into its eyes and stroked its feathers before turning to them. He walked over to Willa, who looked curiously into his eyes.

"Horace? Are you ..." she faltered.

He smiled, sighed. "Yes. I'm back. For the moment anyway." He held out his arm, offering her the bird. "The phoenix is yours, Willa. She has risen from the ashes of her mother, and will live and thrive until it is her turn to die in the flames and give birth to the next generation."

The bird hopped onto Willa's arm and shook its wings. Willa coughed as soot and ashes showered over her. The others laughed.

"So ... what's next?" It was Tengu.

Willa was already nodding, deep in thought. The words spilled out. "Mab can start her knitting again, if we can find her some needles. Then we can go back ... Robert, Mab, and the tree nymphs can hide in the stable. We'll need to find a chair for Belle, and —"

She suddenly stopped, remembering Miss Trang was back. She glanced sheepishly up at her. "Oh, I'm sorry, I ..."

Everyone was grinning at her, which made her blush wildly. Miss Trang too was smiling fondly at her, which made Willa more than a little nervous.

"No, that's all right, Willa. You have everything under control."

Willa wasn't sure if Miss Trang was mocking her, but it didn't sound like it. So she drew a deep breath, and her voice was steady and assured. "Right. Baz, look for a chair and a blanket for Belle. Mab, see what you can dig up for knitting needles. Horace, you and Robert see to the stable. And Tengu, help me hide Dinah!"

Dinah seemed happy enough to descend into her old home in the pool, out of all the excitement, and they laid the big blue tarp over her. Robert made himself comfortable in the stable. Baz found a blanket to cover Belle, but her wheelchair was lost in the blaze. The best that could be done was to roll her about in a wheelbarrow, which, surprisingly enough, did not elicit the slightest complaint from Belle. Mab was reunited with her wool and the wood nymphs helpfully fashioned a pair of knitting needles out of wood splinters. As Mab began to knit, Willa dashed to the front of the burning house.

The flat grey around them dropped like a curtain and the outside world loomed forward, its colours painfully vibrant. People in the street jumped back in shock, pointing at the house. Some ran off shouting. By the front walk Willa saw her mother slowly rising from the ground, looking up fearfully, but the birds were gone.

"Mom! MOM!"

Willa streaked toward her, threw her arms around her and buried her face in the fuzzy housecoat.

"Willa, honey, it's all right. Everything's all right," her mother cooed. Willa lifted her head and looked thoughtfully up at her mom. Her mother started in surprise, put a hand to Willa's hair.

"What? What is it?" Willa felt her hair as the others congregated around them, Tengu pushing Belle in the wheelbarrow, and Robert absent of course. Baz held up a large shard of broken window for Willa to see her reflection in. There was a wide streak of silver running through her hair. Willa laughed.

"I look like the Bride of Frankenstein!"

Her mother put a hand to her own hair. "We can fix that up." Belle gave her a sharp, disapproving look. Willa looked at the two women frowning at one other another, and, as the sound of fire trucks wailed in the distance, she smiled.

"It's time to go to the ocean."

Chapter Seventeen

The sea

Around midnight they set out. Miss Trang managed to conjure up a very thick fog, but Willa was still anxious that they might be seen and had her fingers crossed for the entire trip. Willa, Baz, Tengu, and Horace rode on Dinah, not the most comfortable ride, as she lumbered across town, her head swinging low over the pavement. Robert trotted alongside with Belle on his back and Mab up on his head. Conversation was light-hearted and friendly for a change. The old folk seemed to have forgotten all their former grievances. They joked and smiled warmly at each other. It was weird. Miss Trang walked alone behind them, quiet and thoughtful.

Willa looked up. She was just able to make out the dark form of the new bird, the phoenix, gliding back and forth above them. She felt a pang of grief for Fadiyah. It was like there was an aching gap in the world now, or at least in her world. She felt alone.

They were all tired, dead tired. The rest of the day had been a bit of a blur. The firefighters could not save the house, it was too far gone by the time they arrived. All they could do was spray water on the blackened remains until every last tendril of smoke had disappeared. Somehow Miss Trang had been able to herd them away from the centaur in the stable, the fairy woods, and the tarpaulin-covered dinosaur. And luckily Willa spotted the bedraggled hibiscus before the firefighters could trample it under their big boots. She carried it carefully to the woods, replanting it and patting down the earth around it. The wood nymphs were uncharacteristically sweet, swarming briefly around her head and giving her faint little pecks on the cheek.

Out front the neighbours gathered, chattering excitedly and marvelling at how quickly the house had gone up. Mr. and Mrs. Hackett circulated through the crowd, speaking darkly of mysterious goings-on to anyone who would listen, but nobody took them too seriously. At dusk the fire trucks rolled away, signalling there would be no more excitement here today, and the crowd reluctantly withdrew as well.

Now, under cover of night and fog, they were on their way to the ocean. After an hour of walking the city disappeared behind them and the ocean's soothing pulse grew louder and louder. They felt a cool breeze coming in from the water. Dinah's pace quickened. The fog fell away and the full moon shone on them like a spotlight as they stepped onto the beach. Willa looked around nervously, but they were in luck. There was no one in sight.

The ocean shone before them, glittering and vast. Dinah paused just long enough for everyone to slide off, her feet shuffling impatiently. Willa gave her a last hug and looked into the huge, moist eye. Dinah bobbed her head a couple of times and turned away, wading out to sea.

The rest of them stood quietly on the shore, watching as Dinah's head grew smaller and smaller.

Willa looked up at Miss Trang. "What will happen to her?"

"I'm not sure. She was certainly out of her element here ... most likely was swept up somehow in our time talisman. Out there she may find her way back to her own world. The ocean lives by its own rules, time-wise."

Willa could see Belle urging Robert forward, her eyes shining with excitement. Robert grumbled about the cold but waded in until Belle was able to slide off, clothes and all, into the waves with a splash and a happy shriek. In a moment her head popped up again, her hair glittering silver in the moonlight as she swam.

Willa turned back to Miss Trang, curious. "So ... you didn't know Dinah was in the yard at all?"

Miss Trang shrugged. "Oh, I knew something was back there but I never got around to taking a closer look." She looked a little sheepish. "It *was* on my to-do list, along with repainting the place and getting the roof reshingled." Here her voice became a sigh. "Won't have to worry about those things now."

Willa turned to look up the beach. She could just make out the shape of her grandfather's little house, but there was no light on. Out in the water Belle had vanished from sight. Willa gasped. "She's gone!"

Miss Trang just smiled. "Oh, I think she's too fond of Baz's scones to leave us. Besides, Belle's only part mermaid now." Miss Trang looked down at Willa. Her voice faltered a little. "I haven't ... thanked you properly for looking after them for me. You ... you did a good job."

She looked away again. Willa smiled. She knew that was probably as much praise as Miss Trang ever gave to anyone. The others sat in the sand, waving to Belle, who had re-emerged, happily swimming back and forth.

Willa glanced nervously down the beach once more. An indistinct figure walked slowly toward the ocean, stopping at the silvery waterline. Willa held her breath. It was her mom. She hadn't seen them, not yet — she was gazing out to sea. A small rowboat soon appeared, Grandpa pulling at the oars, his back to them. As Willa watched, he stopped rowing and quietly shipped his oars, gazing up at the brilliant moon.

The group fell silent. Belle had spotted him too, her head barely above the water as she swam silently toward him. Then with a flip of her tail, she dove under the boat. Willa held her breath. After what seemed an eternity there was a silvery flash, and another and another. Grandpa cried out in astonishment as fish, dozens of them, leaped out of the water, soaring right into his boat, a glittering waterfall of fish. The rhythmic thunking sound could be heard from shore. Grandpa turned, looking all around, finally spotting Belle's head in the water. They stared at each other for a long time.

Willa felt tears in her eyes. "Thank you, Grandma," she whispered.

Behind her she heard Baz mutter, "Oh, you poor dear." And up the beach she saw her mother turn away and disappear into the dark trees.

Willa kicked off her shoes and took a couple steps into the water. It was cold. Between waves she caught glimpses of herself in the water, the silver in her hair shining in the moonlight.